BEAUTY AND SADNESS

BEAUTY AND SADNESS

Or the Intermingling
of Life and Literature

ANDRÉ ALEXIS

ANANSI

This edition published in 2010 by
House of Anansi Press Inc.
110 Spadina Avenue, Suite 801
Toronto, ON, M5V 2K4
Tel. 416-363-4343
Fax 416-363-1017
www.anansi.ca

Distributed in Canada by
HarperCollins Canada Ltd.
1995 Markham Road
Scarborough, ON, M1B 5M8
Toll free tel. 1-800-387-0117

House of Anansi Press is committed to protecting our natural environment.
As part of our efforts, this book is printed on paper that contains 100%
post-consumer recycled fibres, is acid-free, and is processed chlorine-free.

14 13 12 11 10   1 2 3 4 5

Library and Archives Canada Cataloguing in Publication

Alexis, André, 1957–
Beauty and sadness / André Alexis.

ISBN 978-0-88784-750-9

1. Alexis, André, 1957–. 2. Literature — Appreciation.
3. Creation (Literary, artistic, etc.). 4. Authors, Canadian (English) —
20th century — Biography. I. Title.

PS8551.L474Z463 2010   C818'.5409   C2010-902001-4

Jacket design: Bill Douglas at The Farm
Text design and typesetting: Sari Naworynski

Canada Council   Conseil des Arts
for the Arts   du Canada

ONTARIO ARTS COUNCIL
CONSEIL DES ARTS DE L'ONTARIO

*We acknowledge for their financial support of our publishing program
the Canada Council for the Arts, the Ontario Arts Council, and the
Government of Canada through the Canada Book Fund.*

Printed and bound in Canada

For Adrina Ena Borde

CONTENTS

Marcher sur les deux rives d'une rivière est un exercise pénible.
— Henri Michaux, "Au Pays de la Magie"

To walk on both shores of a river is a painful exercise
— Henri Michaux, "In the Country of Magic"

INTRODUCTION

I began to write *Beauty and Sadness* as I was finishing a novel called *Asylum*. I had originally planned a series of critical essays on literary subjects, but as I wrote my first essay, the idea of criticism began to perplex me. I've been a contributing reviewer to the *Globe and Mail*'s book section for some time. I take the consideration of works of fiction as a happy duty, a chance to reflect on things I love: literary universes, worlds of words. But it occurred to me that in doing the kind of reviewing I've done in the past — read, reflect on, draw conclusions about a novel or collection of short stories — I was stuck in a voice.

When I began writing reviews, the most difficult thing was to say what I meant in a tone and manner that didn't sound pompous or peremptory. I wanted a voice that was considerate and genuine. And I found that voice, I think. The problem is, *that* voice was the one I instinctively adopted when I began writing *Beauty and Sadness* and, after a few paragraphs, I realized I'd grown tired of it. It works well for reviews, but I wanted something different for a book of essays. I began to think about other ways of paying attention to the literary "object." It wasn't only about finding a new voice. I wanted an approach that would allow for a different kind of attentiveness. That's when I wrote the first of the pieces in this collection, "Maupassant."

The process wasn't quite so straightforward. "Maupassant" first came into being when I read an article about the Welsh musician John Cale. At the end of the article, Cale mentioned a story by Guy de Maupassant in which a man is attacked and killed by his furniture. Lovely idea, I thought. I must read the story. So, I combed through the complete stories of Maupassant. It was a pleasure, a return to work I admire, but I never did find Cale's Maupassant and to this day I don't know if Cale had misremembered the author or misremembered the story or simply invented it all. I liked Cale's account of the story so much, however, that I decided to use it. I wrote my version of John Cale's version of a Guy de Maupassant story. The result, aside from being what I hope is an interesting piece, was an exploration of what I knew or felt about Maupassant's sensibility.

In writing the story, I found myself paying attention to Maupassant and I wrote something that is macabre, supernatural, and slightly off: just the qualities I love in Guy de Maupassant's strongest stories — "La Horla," for instance.

For the second piece, I decided to repeat the process. This time, though, I used elements from the work of Jean Cocteau — poetry, the underworld, Orpheus, and the love Orpheus's Death feels for him. Most of these come from Cocteau's film *Orphée*, but Cocteau's love of poetry, the mysticism of poetry that pervades his work, is what moved me as I wrote. With this story, I was even more aware of sharing the page with another writer, with Jean Cocteau, of working with some of his materials and, in this way, of both distorting and preserving something of Cocteau as he exists within me. I was, in other words, writing my version of Cocteau, using fiction to translate and criticize — in the sense of bringing forward or elucidating — the work of a writer whose films and prose have given me great pleasure.

As I wrote "Cocteau," I also became aware of my imagination as a kind of medium through which ideas are seen or through which they move. I distorted, perhaps even perverted, the ideas I took from Cocteau. The result is like the distortion that happens when you see something in clear water: aspects of an object curve strangely, appear larger than they are, refract when the surface ripples.

And so it is with most of the pieces in *Beauty and Sadness*. In each of them, some aspect of the writer under consideration (Guy de Maupassant, Jean Cocteau, Henry James, Yasunari Kawabata, Leo Tolstoy, Dante, Samuel Beckett) is refracted or distorted. At the same time, of course, you'll be aware of the element that is my imagination, and that, too, is essential. Well, unavoidable, anyway, because this is a collection of essays/fictions written from my perspective and sensibility.

The most difficult stories to write were those based on Kawabata and Henry James.

In the case of "Kawabata," I used what I remembered of a fictional world I adore. I tried to recreate Yasunari Kawabata's aesthetic as I remembered it. I avoided rereading him. I took nothing directly from Kawabata but my memory of his tone and his ways of looking. I worked to keep "André Alexis" at a distance. What made the process difficult was just this wilful rejection of my own sensibility. I could not be absurd or ironic in my way. I couldn't be quite so "interior." (Though, on rereading Kawabata's work after writing the story, I discovered how absurd, ironic, and interior he actually is — try the *Palm of the Hand Stories*. In rereading his work, I discovered how deeply his sensibility had influenced mine, without my being aware of it.) Yet, if

"Kawabata" was one of the most frustrating things I've attempted, it was also the most intimately rewarding. In trying to keep myself out of the writing, I came to see my own style and approach more concretely, recognizing my usual swerves by trying — though not always succeeding — to avoid them.

The Henry James piece was difficult for other reasons entirely. In fact, it is, judging by the rules I set out for this collection, a failure. I began, hopefully enough, with a number of Jamesian elements: a young woman in Paris, an instance of the supernatural, a narrator whose perversity is understated but notable. In working with these elements, however, my Jamesian "essay" was sideswiped by Carlos Fuentes's *Aura*. I hadn't thought about *Aura* for years. (It is, along with Yuri Olesha's *Envy* and Venedikt Erofeev's *Moscow to the End of the Line*, one of my favourite short novels.) But, for some reason, the atmosphere I'd written was suggestive of *Aura*'s atmosphere and my story's narrator, though he is not at all like Fuentes's, brought the narrator of *Aura* to mind. (This is, perhaps, because *Aura* is Fuentes's most Jamesian work.) For a week or so, I was completely blocked. I desperately wanted to write a Henry James narrative that would fit in with this collection, but I felt the story itself wanted to be its own creature. Remembering how strong the second-person voice was in *Aura*, I rewrote the story — now called "Mylène Saint-Brieuc" — in the second person, and it felt . . . right, somehow. It is a piece midway between what I remember of *Aura* and the remembered pleasure I've had with a number of James's novellas and short novels (my favourites being *Turn of the Screw, Daisy Miller, What Maisy Knew,* and *The Sacred Fount*). "Mylène Saint-Brieuc" is a hybrid and, for that reason, probably doesn't belong here. And yet, as the story is the product more of my literary imagination than of my personal vision (insofar as those things can be segregated), it isn't entirely out of place, either.

But why the subjects I've chosen? Why Cocteau or Maupassant? Why not Dostoevsky, E. T. A. Hoffmann, or Raymond Queneau, writers who've had a deeper effect on my imagination?[1] The answer is, first, because one rarely has a chance to deal with writers one admires who *haven't* been major influences. One is usually asked to comment on work that has had some fundamental effect on one's life or art. But there are so many works of fiction (or poetry) that have given me

---

1 And why no black writers? I am a black writer myself. It feels rather like hiding to leave out Ralph Ellison or Buchi Emecheta. The answer to this is relatively simple, though. I had planned to write an essay on black Canadian literature for *Beauty and Sadness*. But as I wrote the final piece in this collection, "Water: A Memoir," I realized I wasn't interested in merely mentioning a few black writers and giving my opinions of them. I want to think — at length — about Ishmael Reed and Leopold Senghor, Toni Morrison and Claire Harris. The subject of race and literature is too vast. It needs its own book, not a few pages in this one. So, I have saved my thoughts and feelings for a second volume of essays.

intense joy *without*, for all that, leaving a deep mark. And it was wonderful to revisit some of the sites of that more fleeting pleasure. The other reason for choosing the writers I did was that I have come to a time in my life when leave-taking, death, and change have begun to seriously impinge on my imagination. Each of the authors I've chosen has dealt with death, the spiritual, the inconstancy of being. *Beauty and Sadness*, which takes its name from a novel by Yasunari Kawabata, is a collection of elegies. It is also an attempt to see over the fence of my own imagination, to look beyond the self into other worlds.

I am an immigrant. I was born in Trinidad and came to Canada when I was four. The process of coming to know this country's geography, its sounds, and its ways of dying . . . that process is mirrored in the literary process I used here. I explore literary worlds and use unfamiliar literary symbols as I explored Canada — this mysterious system of symbols — when I first came to the country. *Beauty and Sadness* is a work of geography as much as it is one of "criticism," if you accept that there are countries named Cocteau, Kawabata, Maupassant, and so on.

The second half of *Beauty and Sadness*, called "Reconciliations," is different in approach and tone. Two of the three essays in the second section — "Ivan Ilych: A Travelogue" and "Samuel Beckett, or On

Reconciliation" — are, on the surface, closer to traditional criticism, but they are essentially travel essays. Their objective is to return to the place they set out from, having followed unusual paths and byways in the work under consideration. Both pieces play with voice and narrative. And both are elegiac. "On Reconciliation" uses the work of Samuel Beckett as pretext for reflection. "Ivan Ilych: A Travelogue" uses Tolstoy's novella *The Death of Ivan Ilych* as its point of departure, though it's as much an exploration of André Alexis's ideas of death as it is of Tolstoy's.

I hate speaking of myself in the third person but, in this book, "André Alexis" is not quite me. Aspects of my life — rather *personal* aspects of my life — have been given to the voices who narrate these pieces on Beckett and Tolstoy, but I have not hesitated to lie or stretch the truth about myself whenever it suited my needs. The point, for me, is the exploration of "other countries." I myself, my concerns, my intellectual and emotional realities will, inevitably, make their appearance, but *Beauty and Sadness* is not, until its final piece ("Water: A Memoir"), autobiography. I have made use of my life in order to look at literary worlds. But I've tried to avoid using literary worlds as pretexts to exposing truths about myself. Which is a long-winded way of saying that, if at all possible, you should regard any "I" you find here with friendly suspicion.

The book's final essay, "Water: A Memoir," is a look at the "literary scene" in Toronto. It is *entirely* personal, an autobiography, as I said. Here, though, I've used the work of my contemporaries, various encounters with writers, and my dissatisfactions and disillusionments as ways to explore the city I've lived in for half my life: Toronto.

Though the two halves of *Beauty and Sadness* are distinct, they are more like mirror images than strangers. This is a book of literary worlds, literary speculations, meditations on literature. It is an illustration of how life and literature intertwine; and it is a (sometimes melancholic) homage to fiction and poetry.

One last note . . .

The four pieces that incorporate aspects of other writers' sensibilities or works ("Maupassant," "Cocteau," "Mylène Saint-Brieuc," "Kawabata") are, more or less, the same story told four ways: a man confronts an avatar of death or chaos and is made aware of something within himself. It's a story that can be told a million ways, of course, but it is also, I think, a model of the critical endeavour. The critic[2] confronts something

---

2   I don't consider myself a "critic." I am a practitioner of an art form — fiction — who explores literary worlds not so much to assess and catalogue, though I do assess and catalogue, as to situate himself, to decide where he belongs or where he wishes to go. The criticism of a Northrop Frye or a Kenneth Burke is beyond me, because in order to do the art, in order to write fiction, one must be ignorant in a way that is, I think, contra-critical.

that, in the best of cases, disturbs his or her soul. It's the cause of this disturbance — the book, the poem, the story — that he or she tries to understand, to situate within his or her life. Though they follow their own paths, the essays that resemble "normal" criticism ("On Reconciliation" and "Ivan Ilych") and the memoir ("Water") are very like the first four pieces. They are about encounter and disturbance, and they are elegiac.

If I have any one hope for *Beauty and Sadness*, it's that these pieces and essays will draw readers to the works of writers I've admired. In the end, this book is my own particular, and maybe peculiar, act of reverence for fiction and poetry.

PART ONE: ECHOES

MAUPASSANT

Perry Anderson had conscientiously done what was expected of him.

He'd learned all there was to learn about the coming trial, for fraud, of his former colleague and friend Mark Beaumont. He would be testifying against Mark, but his part was relatively straightforward. There was record of an unexplained transfer of some two hundred thousand dollars to a personal account held by Mark himself. All Perry had to do was bear witness. He had only to tell the truth, to answer the most basic of questions.

It had been annoying, going to Toronto to be briefed. It was always tiresome visiting what he thought of as an oddly hellish city. And he rather resented the time spent away from his wife (the very thought of her brought images of white cotton sheets and the sea sound of parted bedclothes) and his children (two wonderful girls: Imogene and Zelda). But in the end, of course, he had dutifully spent his days in Toronto being briefed by a lawyer and attending meetings with the company's board of directors. Now, his "prepping" over, and having called his wife to let her know he was on his way home, and having spoken with both of his girls, he was at Union Station waiting to board the train to Ottawa.

Though he had seen Union Station countless times, had explored its underground concourse and wandered in its tall-ceilinged near-grandeur, he almost always found the station off-putting. It wasn't church-like. It was too impersonal for that. Rather, it was a place in which the sacred was perpetually frustrated. He preferred Ottawa Station. There was nothing special about Ottawa Station. It was only a pause on the way home.

At the announcement that first class was boarding, Perry picked up his modest suitcase and went to track 11. He was directed to the first-class car and he found his seat easily enough. The problem was that an old woman, thin, her hair chalk white, was ensconced in his place.

— I'm sorry, he said, but I think you're in my seat.

— Oh, she answered. Am I? I don't think so.

— Well, said Perry. My ticket says 14B and that's the seat you're in.

— I'm certain this is my seat, young man. You could sit somewhere else, you know.

— Why don't you let me see your ticket, said Perry. I think we can straighten this out.

— I really don't want to move, she answered. I'm simply too old.

The steward approached.

— Is there a problem? he asked.

— No, no, said the old woman. There isn't a problem. This young man is only confused, that's all.

The train was full, but it was not overbooked. The seat in question, which was undoubtedly Perry's, was not beside a window, not close to an exit, not neighbour to the toilet. There was nothing special about it. There was no clear reason for the old woman's intransigence. Of course, at some point, the elderly abandon their commitment to reason, don't they? As if speaking to a foreigner, the steward slowly and clearly said

— May I see your ticket please?

— Why do you want to see my ticket?

— If you don't show me your ticket, I'll have to have you taken off the train. Do you understand?

— There's no need to get shirty, young man. My ticket is right here.

The steward, visibly annoyed at being called shirty, said

— Your seat is 15A. It's the next row back.

If the steward was unsympathetic, it was because he'd had recent experience with the wilfulness of the aged. The day before, between Kingston and Smiths Falls, an old man had cursed him for handing him a package of "stale peanuts." This woman was an "old bat," he thought. And then, suddenly aware of the strangeness of the cliché, he smiled crookedly. Why, after all, should we call old women bats and not, say, flies or snakes or goats? No, "goats" was for old men. And that suddenly seemed amusing too, bats and goats being an odd pairing. So, amused by a will-o'-the-wisp, the steward smiled again, a smile the old woman took for complicity.

— I really am very comfortable here, she said. I don't want to move.

The steward turned to Perry and shrugged as if to ask

— Is this all right with you? What would you like?

The old woman looked, it seemed to Perry, smug and petulant. He was inclined to insist on his proper seat but, had he discomfited her, he would not have been able to enjoy the journey home.

— It's fine, he said. I'll sit in 15.

He picked up his suitcase and put it in the compartment above row 15. 15A was a window seat, an improvement, if you liked window seats. And, in a way, he did, the countryside being, from Port Hope to Kingston, so dull it inevitably put him to sleep.

6

The place beside Perry's was occupied by a short man dressed entirely in black: black shoes, pants, shirt, and dinner jacket. He seemed fascinated by a deck of cards he fanned and contracted. He looked up, caught off guard by Perry's presence.

— Are you sitting by the window? he asked.

— I am, yes, answered Perry.

The man stood up to let him by, and when Perry had settled in his place, the man said

— It's certainly a lovely day.

He said it without irony, though it was raining and the day was like a grey sheet pulled over the face of Earth.

— A good day for ducks, Perry answered.

But the man was back at his cards, fanning and contracting them, as though his were the only deck to which this could be done. Perry felt immediate dislike, not because there was anything inherently unlikeable about his travelling companion, but because Perry had — had since childhood — an intense dislike for magicians. So, he turned away from the man and kept his mind on the landscape.

The train made its way through Prince Edward County: the lake gunmetal grey, its white furls making it look like peeling wallpaper, the rocky shore wet and brown, the green trees leaning with the wind. The trees leaning

. . . the shore obscured by the grey of day . . . the horizon vague, like a half-heard suggestion . . . and him asleep already with the sound of the train in his ears: cocoon in cocoon in cocoon in cocoon . . .

— My name's Michael. And yours?

In his imagining, Perry turned his head to his neighbour and, on the verge of waking, answered

— Perry.

— Nice to meet you, said Michael. Listen, I wonder if I could impose on you a few minutes? I've got an engagement in Ottawa and I'd like to practise a little.

And he held out his deck of cards, black backed with a white skeleton in the centre and a red *D* on the skeleton's forehead.

Wearily, unhappily, Perry took a card: queen of diamonds.

— Tear it up, said Michael.

And this, with some difficulty, Perry did.

— Good. Now, look in your breast pocket.

Perry did. There was nothing there but lint and a lime green (and strangely moist) chit from the dry cleaners.

— Christ on a cross! said Michael. I have the worst luck.

Perry searched through every one of his own pockets. Nothing. Michael then searched himself and, after asking the people around them to pat their pockets for a card, found the queen of diamonds in the pocket of the old woman who'd taken Perry's seat. The woman was frightened when Michael leaned over the top of her seat, and, when his elbow hit her in the forehead, upset.

— I do apologize, said Michael. I'm a magician.

Perry looked at him for the first time: thin verging on emaciated, a charmless, beardless face, blue eyes, large hands with long fingers, the whole of him caught in clothes that were a size too big. As with all magicians, there was something unhealthy about him.

— I know, said Michael. I'm lousy at this, aren't I?

Perry politely demurred.

— No, no, he said. It was still quite a trick. It just went a little wrong.

— Things like this just seem to happen to me, said Michael. Last year I was at a birthday party. I was supposed to change cake into cream. Pretty good trick, I thought. But I turned the milk into cake and then they had to Heimlich this poor child. It was just dreadful. But, enough about me. What do you do, Perry?

— I manage a department store.

— Really? What's that like?

— Long hours, but I still have time for my family.

— That's the spirit. No family, no soul, I always say.

— Do you have a big family?

— No, said Michael. I don't have a soul, I'm afraid. But let me try this trick again. Do you mind?

Reluctantly, Perry picked another card from the deck — ace of diamonds — and ripped it up. Michael tried to have it appear in Perry's pants pocket only to have it appear (again) on the person of the old woman. Perry refused to pick a third card. In fact, were it not for the embarrassment Michael expressed, he would have taken offence, it being clear that the card could not simply manifest on the old woman without the magician's will, and he was beginning to feel sorry for the old lady.

— This is all so humiliating, said Michael.

— Do you do something *other* than magic?

— You mean, given my incompetence? Well, I study theology at St. Michael's, but I've always wanted to be an entertainer. You wouldn't believe it, but I can usually get things to go where they're supposed to, you know.

Still unsure if he were being put on in some way, Perry asked a few questions about theology. Why had Michael chosen it? (He was fascinated by the idea of "god.") Was it difficult? (It *was* hard to tell Peter of Ghent from Julian the Apostate, or to remember why transubstantiation was a problem for Protestants. But it was endlessly entertaining.) Whom did he admire? (St. Anselm, above all, because he was amusing.) None of this meant anything to Perry, who had studied commerce. But it all sounded like the kind of thing a theology student might enjoy.

Unfortunately, his questions led to tedious conversation. Michael was entranced by the minutiae of God, and his knowledge of minutiae was bewilderingly broad: from Augustine's assertion that the Lord's fingernails would not need cutting to John of Antioch's belief that, a beauty spot being by its nature an imperfection, God could not have one. Who knew that men and women had spent so much time meditating on the particulars of the holy body?

For what seemed hours, Michael talked on and on, and Perry, with decreasing patience, nodded politely, the only interesting moment coming when Michael asserted that men were, by their nature, demonic.

— No, said Perry. I don't agree.

— You haven't thought it through, said Michael. Men worship the thing they're not, okay? And since they worship God and the good, it follows they're neither godly nor good. In my book, that makes them satanic, you follow?

— I don't know anything about it, said Perry. I wonder if you'd mind if I slept for a little while. I'm tired.

Perry turned to look at the landscape as it flew by: the weeds by the side of the tracks (chicory, goldenrod, purple-headed thistle), the rocks and trees, the fields and farmhouses, and then the lake, somewhere in the distance, its presence palpable. If there had to be a God, he would as soon worship the land itself.

And then came the announcement for Smiths Falls. (So soon? Where had Kingston gone?)

They had stopped in the station. Someone descended from the train. Then they were off again. Beside him, Michael was now doing something with a black handkerchief, pushing it into his left fist with his right index finger, extracting it from his own nostril.

— Say, said Michael, have you seen this trick before? It's the only one I've really mastered. I know it's a little off-putting pulling it from my nose, but, you know, one of my friends pulls it from his . . . ears, to use an anagram.

It suddenly occurred to Perry that the old woman had known exactly what she was doing when she'd refused to sit by this tiresome little man.

More sharply than he intended, he said

— Look, that's enough. Just let me read my book, will you?

— But you don't have a book, said Michael smiling.

And reaching into the pocket of his raincoat where he'd (optimistically) put a Ross Macdonald, Perry found a thick, white card on which was printed, on one side:

Cabeça vazia é oficina do diabo

and, on the other:

An empty head is the devil's workshop

It had been a mistake to indulge the man. He should have stopped him after the first card trick.

With the simple-minded, it was best to get out of the way as soon as possible. And he could see from Michael's smirk that he was simple-minded. He was either that or malicious. Whichever it was, Perry had had enough.

— Give me back my book, he said.

— Oh, said Michael. I can see you're annoyed. Let me get it for you. I'm pretty sure the old woman has it.

Without warning, Michael reached over to the old woman's seat and extracted, without looking, from somewhere on her person, Ross Macdonald's *The Ivory Grin*. The old woman gave a strangled cry.

— There you are, said Michael. But, you know, you shouldn't put so much value in your possessions. What's a book, or a house, or a car? They're encumbrances, when you think about it. I remember this one story —

— I don't want to hear it, said Perry.

— Let me tell it anyway, said Michael. It's by a Frenchman, and in it a businessman, just like you, comes home one night and there's no one there. The house is empty: no wife, no kids, all the furniture gone. He's stunned. What has happened to his world? He goes outside and, out of nowhere, his furniture approaches, moved by God knows what force, and attacks him. Tables, chairs, credenzas . . . they batter the man to death. And that's it. He's killed by his belongings. I'm sure there's religious significance in there somewhere.

Michael smiled in an unpleasant way, and it seemed to Perry that he was one of those men whose essence is the smirk. He thought himself beyond humanity, beyond the day-to-day that bound his fellow men. It may even be, Perry thought, that Michael was neither simple-minded nor clever but, rather, unfathomable and dangerous. He looked into Michael's face a final time and then took his novel, rose from his seat, gathered his belongings, and, excusing himself, went to the steward.

— I wonder if I could sit somewhere else? he asked. I'm uncomfortable.

— There's a seat beside mine, answered the steward. Is anything wrong?

— No, said Perry. I'm just uncomfortable. That's all.

And that was that. Or no, it wasn't. When Perry had made himself comfortable, when he had begun to read the Macdonald (the words were strangely unstable and the shape of the letters shifted, an *r* at the end of "codger" — or was it "roger"? — wriggled as if it were a child in a car seat before becoming an *s*), Michael approached and, as if chiding him, said

— Here you are. I wondered where you'd gone. You left so quickly, I didn't have time to get my card back.

— What card?

— The five of diamonds.

— I don't have it, said Perry.

Brushing a lock of hair from his forehead, Michael said

— You have it. You just can't find it. But I'll see you again.

To himself, Perry said, Not likely. He did not say it aloud because, of course, one never knew with the unbalanced. Michael bowed, then bowed again more reverently before backing away, a sarcastic smile on his face.

As he often did when he did not have much to carry, Perry took a taxi to the far end of Arrowsmith Drive and walked the rest of the way. It allowed him to, internally, at least, throw off the concerns of the day as he approached home: his wife, his daughters, the piece of land they owned at the end of the road. Moreover, as he almost inevitably made the walk around sunset, there was the pleasure of the coloured sun (pink, orange, sometimes even crimson or red), the darkening blues of the sky, the yellow of the lights in the houses along the street.

This evening was particularly affecting. There was a handful of clouds in the sky and the houses on Arrowsmith looked old and stately, though they were new and common. It was the kind of evening that naturally suggested something or other about God.

Or so it seemed to Perry, who, thanks to Michael, had God on his mind. And it struck him how little he had ever thought of God or the sacred or any such thing. It was possible, wasn't it, to see the world, the world as it was on this evening, as a kind of sacred anteroom, a place where God had recently been, one that still held his presence. He smiled at his own presumption and then thought of Michael and the opposite of God. If the world this evening was a sacred room, what would demonic space be like?

He shuddered as he pushed open the wrought-iron gate to his home and dismissed thoughts of the sacred, the profane, and the demonic. Or, more exactly, these thoughts faded as he approached his house and imagined the look on his daughters' faces, the feel of Zelda's chubby feet, which he would hold as she sat on his shoulders, the smell of his wife's hair and clothes.

The lights in the house were all on. But there were no sounds save those he made, no voices, no hum of appliances, no other footsteps. It was so quiet, Perry looked at his watch to make sure it wasn't much later than the seven o'clock he imagined it to be. The numerals of his watch were blurred, but it seemed to be 7:15. He called out and got nothing but the echo of his own call, an inexplicably resonant echo, inexplicable until he entered the living room and saw that there was no furniture. The house had been emptied of furniture. There were only the white walls, polished wooden floors, stuccoed ceilings, light fixtures with their bulbs. He looked again at his watch, instinctively convinced an answer to all this lay there with the time. It was still *something*:15. No matter how closely he looked at his watch, the numerals would not stay still. It was 7:15, surely.

It briefly occurred to him that Liz might have taken the children and the furniture and fled their marriage without telling him. But the thought was absurd. His and Elizabeth's marriage had never been contentious. In their twenty years together, they had not exchanged more than, at the outside, five minutes' worth of unpleasant words. (Honestly, not more than five, and four of *those* had come during the birth of their eldest, Imogene, whose delivery had been so painful Liz had allowed herself some wounding words about him and his entire sex, words she had taken back hours later.) Besides, he had spoken to his family from the station in Toronto not six hours before. There had been not the slightest tremor of distress in any of their voices.

No, there had to be some other explanation.

Robbery, for instance?

Yes. That was it. They had been robbed by thieves with trucks and enough manpower to strip the house in a few hours flat. Liz and the girls, if they had not been kidnapped, would be hiding at one of the neighbours', waiting for him to assure them the danger was past.

He went from house to house. But although the lights were on all along the street, no one was home or no one answered. By the time he rang at the Rodinsons' house at the top of Arrowsmith, the mystery had deepened and he felt something like the despair he'd felt when Zelda, six months old, had had her first attack of asthma. That is, he felt powerless, as if he were himself a child. As he walked back home, it became a dark night. The stars were confident in their places. The stridulations of the crickets were uninterrupted by the *shhsh* of passing cars.

Perry walked through his house, went out the back door and through the wooden gate that separated their home from the woods into which Arrowsmith jutted. It was ridiculous to look for his family out here at night, but such was his distress that he imagined Liz and the girls hiding behind the trees, waiting for him to give the word that everything was all right. And, at first sight, he thought he had been right. He didn't see either of his daughters or his wife, but he saw his furniture, dozens of pieces neatly arranged in a semicircle at the edge of the woods. Some of the pieces were well in the woods, just visible by the light from Perry's backyard. His rolltop desk, for instance, seemed to be hiding behind a thin poplar, a hippo hiding behind a reed.

Two things occurred to Perry almost at once.

First, he thought he saw someone lying on the living-room sofa. The sofa itself was in the woods beyond the first trees, but as he went to it, he saw it was vacant. A bough had cast an oddly wavering shadow on the cushions. He called his daughters' names and then his wife's, but there was nothing, save the momentary silence of the crickets.

The second thing that occurred to him was that he was dreaming. What brought *this* thought was a bedside table that stood near the sofa. On the table, clearly visible and face up, was a five of diamonds. Rather than inspiring fear or dread, the card brought relief and an irrepressible laugh. He examined it and saw that it was, in fact, *exactly* like Michael's card: dark back, skeleton, red *D*.

It was, of course, impossible that Michael's card should be here, behind his house.

Ergo, though he was lucid, he was dreaming.

Moreover, he knew the course of this dream: he would be attacked and killed by his own furniture. Wasn't that what "Michael" had described? And could there be anything more ridiculous? What would come at him first? The credenza or a lawn table? A kitchen chair or the wooden stepladder his daughters used to reach the bathroom tap?

Really, either it was a dream or he had entered a

place beyond his understanding and, if that was the case, if he was in the midst of something supernatural or demonic, what was there to do but treat it all as if it *were* a dream? On the other hand, the thought of the demonic was, despite his fear, intriguing. It was exhilarating even. What would Satan want of him?

As if in answer to that very thought, Michael stepped out of the woods.

— I can't believe my bad luck, said Michael. The *old woman* was supposed to sit beside me. Not you.

— I didn't know, said Perry.

— It's not your fault, said Michael. I've always thought free will was diabolical, and not in a good way either. But, honestly, Perry, you have no sense of evil. Don't you think Satan has better things to do than rearrange your furniture?

— But you're going to kill me, aren't you?

— It would be a kindness, if I did. The worst you can bring yourself to imagine is the loss of your wife and children. And you can't even do that with panache. I mean, you could have imagined them flayed alive or nailed to the trees, raped or mutilated or any number of things. But, no, in *your* worst nightmare they've simply disappeared. I'm stymied by men like you.

— So, I *am* dreaming, said Perry.

— Yes. But that doesn't mean I won't kill you. I'm capable of kindness, you know. In a few minutes, your furniture will trample you to dust. It's a waste of my talents, but I feel for you, and *someone* has to save you from your well-balanced life.

So saying, Michael touched Perry's shoulder and leg, turned his back, walked out of the light and into the woods. And Perry found himself unable to move. He stood before the semicircle of his belongings, dismayed and frightened as the dark grew darker and there was something like a rumble from the earth. He had heard that when one dies in dreams, one dies in reality as well.

What came at him first was a night table. It moved away from the rest of the furniture and then ran at him. As if on cue, the other pieces came to life. The sofa shook. A floor lamp trembled. And then, preceded by the night table, the chairs, credenzas, desks, lamps, chests, tables, loveseats, recliners, and grandfather clock charged as one, bearing down on him like a herd of wasp-maddened cattle.

A spectacular end, a martyrdom by home furnishing, himself a St. Sebastian of the suburbs, his death one that would be mentioned, speculated on: *how strange . . . how odd . . . he died in his sleep . . . who would have thought?*

But Perry was not that kind of man. He had not lived the kind of life that had a place for maddened furniture, diabolical encounters, or phantom neighbours. And he woke from his dream, relieved and disappointed, as a night table struck his thigh and the steward announced their arrival in Kingston.

— Kingston Station, Ladies and Gentlemen. Kingston.

Beside him, the young man had put his cards away. He was now balancing a coin between the fingers of his right hand. His fingers fluttered and the coin moved from knuckle to knuckle before being passed from little finger to thumb to begin its journey again.

It was unpleasant to watch, but there was nothing diabolical about it.

The small details of life overtook Perry as soon as the train arrived in Ottawa. He gathered his things, negotiated his way around the slower travellers, thinking only of home, scarcely seeing what was before him. He was among the first out of the station, the sky above filled with clouds, though here and there you could see a bright evening through the rents in the cloud curtain.

He took a cab from the station, through the city, to the end of Arrowsmith, from where he walked home. How different this walk was from the one he'd recently made in his dream, though, for a moment as he walked, the worlds coexisted, and it was as if he were walking along the street and a map of the street at the same time.

The houses were lit up, dark outlines with warm yellow patches, and the neighbourhood looked as if it had been waiting for him. In the Rodinsons' living-room window, Mr. Rodinson stood talking to someone out of Perry's view. In an upstairs window at the Ricciardis', a young Ricciardi was practising the violin. The boy's movements were graceful, and you could faintly hear the notes of Vivaldi's *Winter*. Here, the Pattons were watching television and, over there, the Gurneys were doing God knows what.

It was exactly as if Arrowsmith, the street itself, had missed him, and although it was home and he *knew* it was home, there was something troubling in the intimacy, something not quite right. It suddenly seemed to Perry that although he certainly belonged here, belonged to the neighbourhood and to the street, the street was dull and unlovely. It was, he thought, exactly the kind of place where men like him lived and, for the first time in quite a while, he felt despair at belonging.

At the sight of his house, gratitude (like a reflex) descended on him. He felt relief, though he could not rightly see what it was that had upset him: the trip to Toronto or the journey back, a foolish dream or a revulsion at the world that was his?

— I'm home, he called
and dropped his bag on the floor beside the doormat.

— In the kitchen
Liz answered and he went to her.

It sounded as if, on the second floor, a troupe of

acrobats was at play. Hard to believe two little girls could produce such a rumpus. Then, as he and Elizabeth kissed, the sound from the second floor stopped, took up again, and grew louder as the girls raced down the steps crying

— Daddy! Daddy!

— What did you get us, Dad?

— Don't run, he cried

but as they came recklessly towards him, he went down on his knees, smiling, his arms open, waiting for the impact of the two compact bodies. But, here again, an unpleasant thought overtook him. As Zelda launched herself at him, he imagined withdrawing or moving out of the way so she fell to the floor. His daughter, seven years old, *knew* he would be there, knew he would not let anything happen to her. He caught her and held her happily wriggling body in his arms, but he said

— You shouldn't throw yourself like that, Zeezee. You'll fall.

When the girls had been tucked in and kissed goodnight, when he and Elizabeth had washed the dishes and put them away, when they had spoken about their plans for the following day and Liz had made herself a cup of tea and carried it up to the bedroom, where she waited for him, Perry took the garbage out to the backyard.

He turned on the light in the yard and, having put the green bag in a metal bin, he went to the gate and looked out at the woods. The parabola of light from their yard was like a pale yellow cloth on the ground before the first thin trees. At night, it was easy to imagine a sacred world adjacent to this one, a world in which everything human was diminished and every speck of earth was a symbol of the divine or its opposite. It was even possible, at night, to imagine the worlds as porous, the divine (or its opposite) intruding on the banal, though he had no real access to that other world, and only glimpsed it in strange dreams. For the most part, the miraculous seemed to shun him. It had left his life ages ago.

But what a *long* day he'd had.

A night wind blew through the trees, bringing with it a cold that drove him back inside. As he closed and locked the door, the day returned to him in pieces: his pity — or was it admiration? — for Mark Beaumont, his train trip, the ambush by his own furniture, his dissatisfaction with home, unhappily belonging to his little world, himself capable of hurting his own child. It was with thoughts like these, surely, that death entered the world. No, not death. Death needed no entrance because it had no exit. Something else entered: the abyss or despair or . . .

No, he had no words for it. He could suffer from it, but he could not name it. And, further frustrated by his own inarticulacy, he pushed an empty teacup from the kitchen counter. It fell to the floor and broke into four or five big pieces and a dozen smaller ones. He would have left it there too — its pale blue florets against the white tile floor — but there were the girls to think of should they rise early and come down to the kitchen on their own. So, dutifully, resentfully, he swept the pieces into a tidy pile by the back door and, defiantly, left them there.

As he undressed for bed, Liz asked

— Is everything okay? I thought I heard something break.

— A teacup, he answered. It was nothing.

COCTEAU

In the beginning, the town of Redfern was a handful of wooden houses beside a shallow lake. After a while, it accumulated a gas station, a restaurant, and a school for the blind. And then, over three decades: a number of churches, two gas stations, a handful of stores, more schools, and a tower tall enough to be seen for miles across southern Ontario. The tower and the school for the blind were the only things that brought outsiders. The tower had been built of stone hacked from quarries in the Middle East. It was a quarter of a mile wide and almost as high. It had been designed and financed by Samuel Tench, at the turn of the twentieth century. Mr. Tench, wealthy and odd, had been obsessed by the Bible since his childhood, obsessed in particular by the Old Testament, obsessed above all by the story of Babel. And so, the tower was built and maintained, until Tench's fortune was squandered. After which, Tench lived alone in his tower until he died, entombed on an upper floor, unmissed until his body was discovered by one of the young men for whom a night in the tower was a rite of passage: some rum for Mr. Tench, no bedding, no pillows, just night, darkness and nerves.

When, in 1957, the county decided to maintain the tower, to keep it clean for tourists, it was discovered that Mr. Tench, dead for some thirty years, had not quite vacated the premises. He presented himself to the first of the tower's caretakers and asked for milk and gin. The man fled, and so did the one hired after him, and the one hired after that, and so on until the death (*angina pectoris*) of the tower's last caretaker, in 1975. After that, the tower's care was kept to a minimum: a small squadron of janitors — townspeople, mostly — who worked at noon. From time to time, young men (and, as the years passed, young women) still tried to spend a night in the tower, but no one went with pleasure, it being almost certain they would encounter the dead. The fortunate ones were kept from entering by the town's lone policeman, who sometimes stood watch until midnight or one in the morning. The less fortunate suffered, each in his or her own way, from their meetings with Mr. Tench and passed into adulthood more traumatised than they might otherwise have been.

So, it was contrary to expectation when, in 1987, the county hired Marin Herbert as caretaker to the tower. It was unexpected because, first, Marin was young: twenty years old. Second, he was legally blind, a graduate of Redfern's school for the blind. He saw little more than a murky blur without the bottle-bottom-lensed glasses he had worn since he was old enough to wear glasses. Third, Marin was nobody's idea of robust. He was thin, his arms and legs like sticks pushed into the long bladder that was his torso. (He was hand-some, certainly, but handsome as poets are handsome: darkly, his inner spirit suggesting pain and redemption and dreams of the Hellespont.) He was hired because his mother was on the committee to keep the tower clean, and Marin had been in and about the tower since he'd been old enough to accompany his mother on her rounds. The place held no frights or terrors for him, and its atmosphere, gloomy and ghost-ridden though it was, reminded him of childhood. Also, his uncle was county reeve, a man respected in Redfern, and he approved of Marin's desire to make himself useful. Marin would sweep up the tower's many rooms, watch over the property, and report any youths who tried to enter the place after dark. In exchange, Marin would have lodgings in the tower (a bed, a table, an ewer and bowl, a bookcase) and two hundred dollars a month. No one envied Marin, and no one suspected he would be at his post for long: a month or two at most, until he decided what he wanted to do with his life — that is, what he *really* wanted to do, because what Marin *thought* he wanted was to be a writer, a thing for which almost no one in Redfern had any use. In fact, Father Hayden, the Catholic priest, had spoken to him about it, gently proposing

— Look, Marin, you've got the Bible, source of all truth. Either you'll write the truth, which already exists in the Good Book, or you'll write falsehoods. And the world has enough lies, doesn't it?

— But, Father, answered Marin, even the echo of our Lord's words is wonderful, isn't it?

— Umhmm, said Father Hayden. I recognize Satan's words when I hear them, you know.

Marin's first night in the tower was uneventful. He swept the top floor (the 33rd), ate the chicken his mother had left in a basket for him, wrote a dozen lines on his Braille typewriter, and then, suddenly exhausted, barely made it to his narrow bed, where he fell into a profound and dreamless sleep. His first seven days passed in much the same way: undisturbed by ghosts or apparitions, Marin would sweep one of the tower's floors, retire to his room, write a few lines of verse — lines which, in the morning, he inevitably found drab and prosaic — before falling into deep, dreamless sleep which did not nourish him at all. In the mornings he was as tired as if he hadn't slept. And then, on his eighth evening, as he was typing his day's complement of verse, he felt a presence, someone looking over his shoulder, and then a voice spoke.

— Your poetry is terrible.

— I know, answered Marin.

And as if it were the most natural thing in the world, Marin and the presence with him discussed poetry. Marin's companion insisted that, being dead, she understood what poetry was about. She was inclined to think poetry something the living did that could be understood *only* by the dead, the dead being the only ones with sufficient distance. Moreover, *his* poetry was "off" because he had the wrong attitude.

— Words know when you're afraid of them, said Marin's companion.

— I see, answered Marin

who saw (in all senses of the word) very little. He felt and he heard, though, and when, after an hour or so, the presence left him, he fell asleep, erotically dreaming about an umbrella on a blue-linen bed. When he awakened in the morning, he was as tired as ever, but he found he had written lines that were not at all like his usual work:

> We will wake bruised in the dew
> glass-wet and gleaming . . .

Now, when had he written that, he wondered, and where did the lines lead? Whose poem was he writing, if not his own? If he had been an intellectual, he might have stopped writing altogether until he could figure things out. But Marin went on in the knowledge that, wherever the verses came from, they were more interesting than his own, and, the following night, he followed his routine. He swept up, retired to write, and, for two hours, hours that passed as if they were minutes, he spoke with the presence that occupied the tower with him, a distinctly feminine presence, though he persisted in thinking of her as "Sam." And the following morning, he woke to find he had filled pages with verse:

> I inhabit my body, as if I were a small visitor . . .

They were nothing to do with him, but he recognized his own handwriting and vaguely remembered *thinking* some of the words.

In the weeks that followed, Marin slept and had vivid dreams, but he woke in the morning as exhausted as he'd been the night before. He wrote reams of poetry: pages and pages of lyrics and sonnets, expressing love for the world and anguish at time's passage, feelings he hadn't known he possessed. Also, his visitor began to spend longer and longer sojourns with him. From the hour she had spent on her first night, she moved to two, to three, to six hours, staying with him, finally, the night long. Her conversation was elegant, informed, and even seductive. So much so that, after three months, Marin began to feel longing for a woman he knew to be dead. Naturally, he found this strange, and found himself strange, too. He was not alone. His mother became concerned at his refusals to leave the tower for more than an hour or so at a time, at his emaciation and pallor. Marin had always been slight, as if, she thought, he could not resolve himself to be part of this world. But, these days, it looked as though he had chosen the hereafter and was headed there. He was dangerously thin, and barely coherent when he wasn't silent. He visited his parents every Sunday, but his mother could tell he was anxious to return to his tower to write, though writing had never taken so much from him before. In distress, she asked the town's only official (that is, published) writer if it were normal for writers to keep to themselves, ignore their families, write until they were pale and exhausted.

— Of course, the writer assured her. I was always exhausted before I was published.

This answer did not reassure her at all, however. It didn't resolve an important matter: Was her son a *real* poet or was Marin wearing himself out with gibberish? Without his permission, she took a handful of his poems and sent them off to a magazine in Toronto. She assumed that his work would be rejected and that rejection would bring Marin to his senses. To her dismay, the poems were accepted and published, but when she told Marin what she'd done, sheepishly congratulating him for his talent, it was as if he couldn't have cared less.

Nor was Mrs. Herbert the only one to notice the change in him. The people of Redfern, most of whom had known Marin since his earliest childhood, were aghast and frightened by his appearance. The same people who had affectionately called him "Stick" now discreetly crossed themselves as he passed. The more cruel called Marin "Death," but they too avoided him, crossing the street to escape his company. Whenever he walked into town to buy water, soda crackers, and chicken soup — his regular diet — Marin was shunned.

He was as preoccupied in town as he was distracted in the tower, however, so Marin did not notice his ostracism.

◌◌◌

For months, much of Marin Herbert's life passed in anticipation of night. Though he was perpetually tired, he could not sleep during the day. An anxiety kept him awake, a fear he might miss the coming of the spirit he loved. He swept the many rooms of the tower or reread the poetry he had written, but for the most part he sat at his desk looking out the window in his room, a window that faced the Baillargeons' cornfield, which, in summer, was a green blur that moved in the wind like a rectangular sea. It reminded him of night. Everything reminded him of night, save night itself, which brought dawn to mind. He would sit at his desk, waiting, and then it was as if the moon had entered and company was there. Marin's vision improved miraculously, to the point where he could see his surroundings clearly, though he was in darkness. He could catch the moths that entered his room to eat the linen of his bedding. More importantly, he could see his companion. She was a foot or two taller than he was, her body covered by a white robe that was loose enough to ripple over her body when the wind blew through the room. She did not smile. She did not seem capable of smiling, nor did she blink. Her stare was intimidating, a quality of attention some might have taken for predatory but for her voice, which was gentle. If he closed his eyes, she was perfectly seductive. No, it was more than that. She was arousing. Whether she spoke of poetry or listened to his words, he found himself overwhelmed by physical desire. And so, Marin kept his eyes open, finding it less shameful to fear than to desire her.

Curiously, this was very like the motive that moved Marin's Death as well. She was even more surprised than he to feel desire. As one who had accompanied countless souls from this world to the next, she had never felt anything like longing. And this was not just longing but something else for which there was no name. Not "love" (that was not her province), not "affection" (she felt affection for all those she'd accompanied), but, rather, a kind of flattered astonishment that Marin could, through his art, speak her name so clearly. She could not actually close her eyes — Death does not sleep — but, if she was not careful, she could lose herself in pleasure. That is, she could be seduced. And so, preferring vigilance to the mystery of seduction, Marin's Death kept her attention on him, moving away when he leaned in her direction. (Once — only once — she carelessly allowed his fingers to brush against the sleeve of her robe, and Marin began to cough as if his lungs had filled with fluid.)

One was wasting away, the other was not of this world. No basis for love, you might have thought. And yet, Marin's Death began to feel precisely that: love, though it was not her province. She began to find it painful to be away from him, though, of course, the longer she stayed with him, the more time she spent looking on him, the sooner his demise would come, and, for the first time in eons, she was not indifferent to a body, not indifferent to breath, and did not long for the last line of the final poem. If it had been his Death's will, Marin would speak her name, over and again, endlessly.

One morning, distracted by her thoughts, Marin's Death left before he was unconscious. The first rays of sunlight were already on the neck of earth, and so it was time for her daily eclipse. She went down the steps of the tower, and when she came to the last of the tower's steps, a further set of stairs appeared, leading down into darkness. Following behind her, dazed, having no object but to remain with her until they had absolutely to part, was Marin himself. He scarcely noticed the change from this world to the next. He entered the underworld as might a man asleep, noticing nothing at first but the increasing darkness, which he took for night. And then, after he'd noticed the dark, he felt the cold. And then, cold, he realized he had lost sight of his Death some time before. And with that, he woke completely and felt the beginning of terror.

No sooner did Marin feel panic, however, than his surroundings were illuminated. He was in a large room, a thousand feet square and a hundred feet tall, and he was not alone. On the far side of the room an old man sat in an armchair . . . or was it a stool? Actually, Marin could not tell what the man sat in because, when he tried to pay attention to whatever it was, it would change: from a bar stool to a Louis XIV loveseat to a rocking chair, and so on. Nor was the chair the only thing that changed. Whenever Marin looked closely at any detail, that detail mutated. The wall nearest him was, at first look, covered in blue wallpaper, then it was wooden, then plain brick, then brick with wainscotting, then . . .

The only stable thing, aside from Marin himself, was the old man, who, having noticed Marin, approached cautiously. From the moment he rose from the thing that accommodated his arse to the moment he stood warily a foot or so from Marin, he was an (oddly familiar) old man.

— You're not dead, said the old man, as if he were aggrieved by Marin's breathing.

— No, said Marin.

— Well, that's just not right, said the old man.

Marin apologized.

— No apology needed, son. It's just I've been trying to get back to my tower and I can't. So, why should *you* be allowed in here?

— Where am I?

— You're in my antechamber. Not very pretty, is it? Ah, but where are my manners? I haven't introduced myself. My name is Samuel Tench. And you are?

— Marin Herbert.

— You're familiar to me. Are you from Redfern?

— Yes. And you're the man who built the tower.

— That I am, lad. That I am, and I'm pleased to meet one of my fellow townsmen. But are you certain you didn't take a wrong step somewhere? My, my, the things that go on. How's my country, lad, and how are my countrymen? It's been some time since I was above ground myself. Not since Death herself decided to move into my home. I've been evicted. You'd expect better from an afterlife, wouldn't you, but there's no relief from suffering, son. I'm more unhappy dead than I was alive.

— Are we in Hell? asked Marin.

Samuel Tench nodded thoughtfully but, after reflection, said

— Not yet, son, but it's our common destination.

— Isn't there a Heaven?

— No, that's just a rumour. Damnation's all there is. That's why I'm staying right here.

— Is there a way out?

— Oh, certainly. There's always a way out.

Pointing to a far corner of the room, Mr. Tench indicated a door Marin had not seen: a door, a portal, a hatch, a curtained exit.

— And this will take me home?

— Home? Yes, lad, it will take you home.

There was something in Tench's tone that should have sounded a warning. The man, or at least the spirit of what had once been a man, looked down at Marin as if Marin were a mouse and he an owl. He raised an eyebrow, smiled, and again pointed to the door.

— There you go, son. Home.

But no sooner had Marin stepped through the door than he understood that he was not home. The door closed behind him and would not open. It was immediately colder than he could have imagined, though his skin was warm. There was darkness, but it was palpable and could be parted so that a bluish light came through. And there were voices, a million of them, each one of which Marin could clearly hear, if only he paid attention to it:

> — *Exhausted after a furious round*
> *of fevered dreams . . .*
> — *Children come and go, wickedly laughing*
> *as they pass . . .*

Does everyone speak verse in Hell? Marin wondered. But he was not in Hell and he heard only what he wished to hear: poetry, his own poetry, though he did not yet recognize it as such. He wandered deeper and deeper into one of the trillion valleys of death, enchanted by the sound of his own words. He was more than enchanted. He was enthralled and would willingly have wandered in the valley listening to his own poetry forever. That this did not happen was because Death came for him. Moving through the darkness like a wind through curtains, Marin's Death found him. She put a hand over his eyes and, holding him by the shoulder, led him back to the world, to morning and to life.

The morning light inaugurated what was to be, for Marin, the interminable end of his life. Waking in his narrow bed in the tower, Marin almost immediately noticed two things awry. First, he could not move his left arm. The point at which Death had touched him, his left shoulder, had deadened. It felt as if his clavicle were driftwood. Second, he could see. His vision was, without his glasses, pure and clean. He could see the cracks and bumps in the tower's walls, could see a silverfish moving on the window ledge. His vision, in other words, had not simply improved. Its improvement had erased the world he had known. Looking out his window at the Baillargeons' field, he could no longer see the rough green lake, but saw instead each of the stalks of corn, their soft ochre tufts.

Though he regretted the loss of his near-blindness, worse was to come. That evening, as he readied himself for his Death, her presence, he was interrupted by the ghost of Samuel Tench.

41

— How are you, lad? Tench asked
surprising Marin by his presence, his tone, and his
appearance — naked, save for a stick-figure drawing of
Satan that was pinned to his chest. No wonder Redfern's youths had been traumatized by the sight of him.
Not traumatized, unimpressed, Marin turned away
from Tench's ghost and wrote. Through the night he
wrote poetry and avoided conversation with Tench, a
premonition of exile making him wary of talk with the
ghost. Tench spoke to him, however.

— My mistake, he said, for directing you to the
place you shouldn't have gone. I feel bad about it. But
it's worked out for one of us, and that's something.
I'm back in my own dear place. No more interfering
from anyone else, either. No one transgresses with
impunity, taking you from the underworld when she
shouldn't have. Well, that's the will of you know who.
Your friend won't be around for a while.

— *When* will she be back? asked Marin.

— That I can't say. No one knows that, except herself and maybe you, in your heart of hearts. She'll be
back when it's time. But whatever do you see in that
sack of ashes, anyway? Life's the thing for lads like you.
You should be out and about in the daytime.

In the months that followed, Marin wrote a thousand poems. He wrote sonnets, villanelles, ghazals,
sestinas . . . all with Death in mind and each more

beautiful than the last. It was as if the dark of night passed through him and into words. Even his parents were now moved by Marin's poems. His father was discreetly proud. His mother, though, wept as she read the pages she collected from the floor of his room. Though she was distressed by Marin's unhappiness, she could hardly believe that her son, the boy whose nose she'd wiped, could write of longing so deep the reading of it brought inexpressible joy. How had her poor, frail son managed to see her soul so distinctly?

In fact, although Marin wrote what he thought of as varied hymns to his Death, wrote every word with her in mind, his work was taken by all who read it as if it had been dedicated to life. Naturally, every reader saw in Marin's work his or her own shade of light, but light is what they saw and Marin was rewarded for it. His first five collections of poetry, each a haphazard gathering of fifty poems, won all the prizes possible. Each sold as if it had been a novel written by some bumbler with a hack-neyed story. That is, they sold unspeakably well. And what an odd situation this created for Marin's peers. What were they to make of such bewildering financial and aesthetic success? Those who sought reputations instinctively loathed Marin and begrudged him the attention. Those who were not so much poets as they were politicians in verse claimed him for their own: Marin as exemplary sufferer. Those who worshipped poetry and language had no choice but to cherish the being through whom poetry and language made themselves known. But whatever the case, whatever the inclination, each and every poet possessed of even a grain of sensibility read him and was moved.

Now, you might think that money, fame, and reputation would compensate for exile and loss: exile from Death's presence and the loss of his only love. They might, had Marin had any of those things in mind while he wrote. However, he did not. And though, for his mother's sake, he occasionally tried to find some happiness in his accomplishment, he most often failed. Worse: as time passed, he grew less and less interested in happiness, failure, success, or defeat. Once the fifth volume of his verse was published, Marin refused to submit another word. In fact, he threatened to burn every page he had blackened, every page he would *ever* blacken, if even so much as a comma of his were published. This left his mother in difficult straits. *She* had submitted his work. *She* had taken care to save his money for him. *She* had become his agent. At his refusal to publish, she had to choose between the pride she felt as Marin's mother, the conviction her son should be compensated for his genius, and a fear of losing a sensibility to which she was herself devoted. After great consideration, she informed Marin's publisher that there would be no further collections. All the while, however, she surreptitiously published a poem here and there in small magazines, using pseudonyms she culled from a Middlesex County phonebook: George Hesketh, Robert van Hie, Nicholas Jaco, and so on. In this way, she fed a trickle of her son's work to the wanting world.

Far from bringing Marin peace or anonymity, his refusal to publish brought ever larger waves of people to Redfern. They came first on foot then by bicycle then by bus — men and women in search of the poet, tramping through Redfern, crowding into the rooms of Tench tower, disrupting the business of the town so much that it was forced to change. In short order, Redfern acquired a new hotel, an old-style antiques shop called Poet's Pickings, a tavern named From Bard to Verse, and a tearoom known as Herbert's Hideaway. The very people who had been frightened of him, crossing the street to avoid his bad spirit, now swore he had always been robust and manly, a scamp with an eye for the women, full-lipped, rouge-cheeked, altogether typical of Redfern. Nor did they want for audiences. The men and women who brought or bought handfuls of Marin's books hung on even the most ridiculous rumours: that Marin had sold his soul to the devil, for instance, shedding a drop of his blood on the Baillargeons' cornfield in exchange for his devilish talent with words.

Marin himself was chased from the tower by the sheer number of visitors. He hid in his parents' basement, abandoning the tower to strangers and to the ghost of Samuel Tench. The tower was overrun by company, and night being the rumoured time to catch Marin while he was writing, the place was packed after midnight. Far from being frightened by a ghost with a stick-figure drawing pinned to his chest, the fanatics who wanted any news or hint of Marin's life began to pester Tench for stories about Marin and his work. So persistent were they that after six months of pestering, and seeing he could no longer frighten anyone, Mr. Tench's ghost decided to take his chances in Gehenna and, one night, vanished from the face of Earth forever. Had Marin been aware of it, this would have been another loss. Though he did not trust Tench's ghost, he had, in the months of nights they had shared, grown accustomed to the ghost's company and, more, was dependent on the late Mr. Tench for proof that there was another world, another world in which the one he loved waited for him.

Now, with Marin living in his parents' basement and with his frustrated followers roaming the streets of Redfern, resentment began to creep into relations between the townspeople and Marin's admirers. Marin's admirers — frenzied, calm, thoughtful, irrational, easily excited, word drunk, poetry mad, considerate, wanting nothing but a glimpse, a lock of hair, a piece of clothing, a moment, an hour, a lifetime — began to feel as if they had been misled. Here was the poet's land and town. Everyone swore Marin Herbert was about, but few could say for certain where he was because very few saw so much as a hair of the man. Some left the town, bitterly disappointed that the man who had seen into their souls refused to speak with them. Others, more unbalanced, began to do damage: knocking post boxes from their stems, bending street signs, breaking windows at the school for the blind.

The townspeople were not entirely unsympathetic. Many of them also felt that Marin's unwillingness to show himself was, at best, thoughtless and, at worst, insolent. Still, there's only so much petty destruction and general misbehaviour a community can take from its visitors. A barrier grew between the townspeople and Redfern's tourists. And amongst Redfern's youth, this barrier was a spur. In the name of "peace keeping," gangs of them rode around in trucks and cars. They rode around from early evening to late night, looking for outsiders who might be up to no good. They carried baseball bats and machetes for show, to intimidate, but as they were teenagers and drank beer while they drove about, they were at least as dangerous as the lovers of poetry sometimes were.

Two years passed: snow, rain, sun, corn harvested, cows milked, calves pulled from the breech, butterflies eaten by birds, mice eaten by owls, death, life, more death, and more life.

The years were not good to Marin. From the moment he abandoned the tower, he felt like a man with a strange affliction. He went out at night, when most of the tourists had gone back to their hotels or bed-and-breakfast inns. He avoided the vicinity of the tower and so avoided most of those who were looking for him. The rest didn't recognize him, because he went out dressed in a suit, tie, white shirt, and cufflinks: nothing like the image of him most of his admirers held, and nothing like the Marin Herbert the people of Redfern were used to.

For two years he did nothing much besides sleep, read, eat, and stare at the furnace as if the answer to a mysterious question were inscribed on it. With the passage of time, he became less and less able to write. His parents' home was simply not conducive to poetry, and though his eyesight had improved, that, too, seemed to work against him: his world was not worth seeing clearly and the sight of it defeated words. Marin's mother encouraged him to write, to go out, to run or paint or anything that might cheer him up. However, in her heart, she found his morosity encouraging. From all she had read — lives of Byron and Pushkin, Baudelaire and Rimbaud — Marin was exactly what great poets were: miserable, unhappy, inconveniently alive. She did her best to comfort him, but she reckoned his discomfort to be part of his process and, in this, she was seconded by the town's other writer, who, these days, spoke darkly of his own misery and, from time to time, tried to finagle an invitation to the Herberts' home to share his pain with Marin. However, as Marin had assured his mother the day would come when he would return to the world, if only he were left alone for a while, Mrs. Herbert never invited "Redfern's other poet," as he was now known, though she did buy his books (*Good Going* and *Twilit Gardens*) and encouraged Marin to read them.

Without knowing it, Marin had in fact told his mother the truth. The day *did* come when he felt the pull of the world, the need to see the fields, to speak with Samuel Tench — whom Marin did not know was twice dead. Two years after his exile, after two years of solitude, grief, and silence, and some six months after he'd last written a word, Marin got up from his cot beside the furnace, washed, shaved, dressed, and resolved to go out into the world.

It was late spring, the perfect time to see the world after a bout of grief and loss, but by the time Marin walked out his front door it was eleven o'clock and dark. The moon was bright, the streetlamps were haloed by a cold mist, and there were two people waiting outside his home, a young woman and a man in his sixties, both of them dressed warmly, talking quietly. At the sight of Marin, the woman stopped talking, stared as he approached, and just managed to ask

— Marin?

before he passed them by.

— Yes? answered Marin.

— It's wonderful to meet you.

— Nice to meet you too, said Marin.

On hearing Marin's voice, realizing that this was the moment he had been waiting for, the man began to cry. He took Marin's hand, kissed it, and, wracked with gratitude, said

— Your work has meant so much to me.

— Thank you, said Marin. Thank you for telling me.

Overwhelmed by emotion, the man and woman stood aside to let Marin pass. They watched as he walked down the tree-lined street, the lights of the houses making the cool spring night seem warmer than it was. Now, how was it that their language had chosen *this* man and *this* land on which or through which to flower? Really, language and ground were such inscrutable conspirators. And yet, the man and woman stood quietly still, their eyes on Marin's back, until he and his black coat disappeared into the darkness.

Marin walked about town, passing the school for the blind, McGregor's greasy spoon, the Catholic church, the Anglican church, the tavern, and Ted's Gas Station before heading to Tench Tower. There were still people about, townspeople and strangers, but no one troubled Marin as he walked, no one stopped him. He was relieved to discover there was no one at the tower: no streetlights, only darkness and moonlight. The tower was strangely blank, less like a building than an impressive heap of stones, but for Marin it was as if he were seeing home for the first time in decades, night making the tower as indistinct as it was in memory.

More: as he stood on the opposite side of the road allowing his emotions to settle, he saw, moving towards him, his Death, her face pale, her eyes open, smiling sadly at him, as if no time had passed since he had unwittingly driven her away. How often, over the years, had Marin regretted his descent to the underworld and cursed Tench for showing him the door he should not have opened. But at the sight of his beloved, his spirits immediately lifted. The years of exile vanished from his mind and soul. In the instant he saw her, he conceived the first words of an elegy, which came to him whole, as if pulled from deep water by its first line.

Ecstatic, filled with love, taking a step towards his Death which came to meet him, Marin Herbert was shattered and killed by the car that struck him.

Two girls and three boys, Redfernians all, stood at the side of the road looking down at Marin's broken and lifeless body.

— What the fuck? You ran over Marin Herbert.

They had been "on patrol," keeping the town safe from wanton tourists. This accident, though, was real trouble. What could you say after killing Marin Herbert? Difficult to answer, even if they hadn't been too drunk to think straight, which they were.

— I didn't know it was him. He stepped right in front of us. You saw it. Besides . . . besides, he hasn't written anything for years . . .

There was much back and forth on the matter. A good half hour was lost, but, after a drunken while, having agreed that they had killed, at worst, the country's *second*-best poet, they cut Marin's body to pieces with a machete and buried it in the Baillargeons' cornfield, which, as luck would have it, had recently been ploughed, so the ground was soft and yielding.

The loss to Redfern was considerable, though not catastrophic. Days after confirmation that Marin had disappeared, when fears for his life were most vivid, Marin's readers came to see if they could find or buy anything of Marin's in Redfern. Then, after six months or so, when it was clear Marin had gone and was, perhaps, dead, and police from all parts of Middlesex County were looking for him, the number of tourists dropped and dropped and dropped again until, a year after his disappearance, a quarter as many people came as had come the year before. Two years after his disappearance, all of his work was published by his mother in the hope that, if he was still alive, he would be peeved enough to call, if only to give her grief — grief which, of course, would have been the sweetest thing imaginable. After that, even fewer tourists came, but those who did were respectful, interested only in the monument to Marin erected in the town centre and in Tench Tower. They did not stay in Redfern for long, but they stayed long enough to keep the tavern, the café, and the bakery going for many years.

In the end, Marin's bones were never found. Every spring there was, when Mr. Baillargeon tilled his cornfield, at least a possibility that the black ground would give up something of the man it had swallowed. That it did not, that it never did, was perhaps proof of a jealousy or selfishness. The world above having Marin's words, the great ocean that was Baillargeon's cornfield kept his remains for itself.

MYLÈNE SAINT-BRIEUC
[HENRY JAMES/CARLOS FUENTES]

When you were younger and better looking, you travelled in Europe. You were, let's say, desirable, and when the money your father gave you ran out, you made your way by trading on your assets. You did well. Your looks, accent, and manners made you attractive. At least, so you were told by the men and women who paid for your travel, lodgings, and meals.

In 1980, on your third trip, you stayed in Paris long after it had quieted down for summer and most of those left on the streets were tourists. You might have done better in Positano or Mykonos, but Paris fascinated you. One afternoon, you walked along the Quai des Grands Augustins, bought a novel by Jouhandeau at a bookstall and, when it began to rain, jogged across the street to one of the brightly lit bistros where you had *rillettes de porc* with a *bâtard*, a *café américain*, and a Pastis. Nothing was good, save the Pastis, but you sat out for hours reading, looking over at the buildings on the opposite bank, admiring the trees and the sunlight behind the grey clouds. In the thirty years since then, you have not been happier, nor more at ease.

That summer was hot, quiet, and expensive. Paris seemed, at times, only a step from stifling, but there was always something amusing to do. There were private clubs open until six in the morning, small theatres, restaurants . . . all things that took money. In fact, you might have run out of money altogether, but it was your good fortune to meet an older woman, Mireille de Saint Something-or-Other, who was wealthy and generous. She had a husband and children, but they happened to be away. And after an amusing night together, she invited you to spend a few days with her in Montmartre, in a many-floored house from whose rooftop garden you could see the jumble of roofs, windows, and chimney pots at the foot of the Basilica of Sacré-Coeur.

You still remember her as she was then. You thought she was "older," but she must have been all of forty. Her hair was light brown, cut so that it looked, perpetually, as if she'd just risen from bed. Her clothes were discreet, until you were close enough to notice how exquisitely they'd been tailored. Her mouth was small, but her teeth were big so that there was always a trace of lipstick on them. Also, though her body was more slack than that of the younger women you preferred, she was compact: small breasts, narrow waist, and a long, narrow back you found fascinating.

Of course, if you remember her body so well it's because she was proud of it herself. For the three days you spent with her, she contrived to be undressed, or nearly so, most of the time. This was pride, in part, but it was also because she'd taken it into her head that you needed an education in the senses. At the time, you found this assumption annoying. You pointed out that your "sensual education" had been at the charge of a number of people, most of whom had paid to teach you. You added that she had shown you nothing you hadn't seen many times before. (You would behave differently now. You now understand how vulnerable she must have felt: a woman alone in an opulent and cold house with a young man she did not know. The fiction that she had something to teach you would have allowed her the illusion of control. But you were twenty-one, and your pride was easily wounded.)

Still, even your good qualities failed you with Mireille. You were, for instance, capable of listening to reams of insignificant talk without seeming uninterested. Her complaints about her husband, whose mistress was "a whore," gripes about her children, who seemed to love their father more than they loved her, endless speculation about her house and its endless renovations . . . You placidly listened to all of it, but you'd had enough of her after your first night, and you had to work to maintain the illusion of interest. To keep yourself alert, you stole what money you found, along with a sapphire ring that was in a bedroom drawer. This thieving was mostly for diversion. You would have given everything back immediately if she'd found you out, because you were not a dedicated thief.

It is difficult to say if Mireille discovered your theft or not. She was the kind of woman who, even if she had, might not have made noise. It would have been inconvenient, for her, to explain your presence to whatever authority she chose. So, it's difficult to be certain. These days, you tend to think she *did* know of your thieving. Though your time was spent engaged in the most intimate ways, a kind of formality grew between you after your second day together, the day you'd stolen the necklace. She still wanted you to do the things she enjoyed, but she was a little colder. That she carried on at all while suspecting you of betrayal may have had something to do with her experience. You were certainly not the first young man she'd entertained in her home. The money and jewellery she left around was, likely, matter she would not miss. In which case, her coldness was, perhaps, a sign of disappointment.

Most telling was your last evening together:

You had spent the day on her large, white bed, playing at a game she liked, one that called for real exertion on your part. And you had played your part particularly well, because her moments of transport were so intense they pulled you right along with her and you experienced memorable pleasure. When you had finished, you both washed in the large, well-lit bathroom. She dried you off in a provocative way and, rather than dressing, you went back to the bed, where, rather than beginning your game again, she wanted to talk.

— My husband is coming home sooner than I thought, she said. I'm afraid we won't be able to see each other anymore.

— *Que lástima*, you said. It's been a pleasure.

— You won't make any trouble for me, will you? I mean, you're not indiscreet.

— No, I'm not. That would be bad for my reputation. Besides, I'm leaving for Formentera in a day or two.

— Are you? That's too bad. I know that you aren't . . . wealthy. I was going to suggest a way you could make a little money, if you wanted.

— One can always use money.

— I have a cousin, she said. Mylène. She has . . . strange needs.

—What kind of strange?

—I don't want to be indiscreet myself, she said. I'll give you her telephone number when you leave. You can tell her that I sent you. Please call me when you've seen her. I'd love to know how she is. I'm so rarely in Neuilly myself.

You kept the name and address of Mylène Saint-Brieuc in the billfold of your wallet for months. Though you sold Mireille's sapphire for relatively little, you had enough money to last until November. You actually *had* meant to visit Formentera, but once again Paris held you. You spent your money in restaurants, or in late-night "boxes" listening to African jazz. You went out with young men your own age, enjoying the sheer, unprofessional amusements of seduction. Though you don't recall many faces from that time, you remember quite a few bodies: pale and young, compact and supple. (These days, the smell of Gauloises can set you thinking about frayed undershirts, long fingers, or late-night bars off rue de la Roquette.)

When your money had again dwindled to nothing, you took the card with Mylène's number from your wallet. You were wary of calling. Enough time had passed for Mireille to have warned her cousin about you. Perhaps Ms. Saint-Brieuc had been told to alert someone—the authorities or men without rules—should you call. Still, you needed money and, besides, the thrill of delinquency was irresistible. So, you called despite your trepidation.

Her voice was small, a young voice, wary. She became slightly warmer at the mention of her cousin's name, but not much. Then, when you told her what it was you wanted, there was complete silence. You thought she had hung up or put down the phone.

— Mademoiselle Saint-Brieuc?

— Yes, she said finally. Just a minute. What is your name, please?

You arranged to meet in Neuilly, not far from her home. You would recognize her, she said, by her beret, if it was raining, or by her hair, if it was not. Her hair had recently been cut and made her look a little severe. If that did not work, you would know each other by your very presence at Place Winston Churchill. No one else would be there so early in the morning: seven o'clock. You couldn't see the point of meeting so early, but Mylène insisted. There were, apparently, conditions or aspects to your transaction, aspects she wouldn't speak about over the phone. There were things you needed to know, "for your own protection." You understood her words, certainly. You were speaking French, your mother tongue. But on the night before you met, you tried to imagine what it was she wished to do to you or what she wished you to do. *Your* protection? The mechanics of lovemaking are usually straightforward. It's the settings, rituals, and boundaries that are the unknown. You decided you would not let yourself be tied up, at least not until you knew she could be trusted.

The woman waiting for you at Place Winston Churchill, by the memorial to the dead, was thin, blue eyed, pale, her fingers long and elegant. She was dressed for November and rain: a white, belted raincoat, black leather boots with small heels, a white umbrella, and a red beret under which she kept pushing a lock of light brown hair that kept falling. She was not at all frightening, not intimidating, and did not seem deranged. After you'd shaken hands, she gave you an envelope in which there were a thousand francs.

— I don't want us to worry about money, she said.

— But we haven't done anything.

— I don't know if we'll do anything at all, but I'm very grateful you came. We can go to La Havane, if you like. I think it's open.

And it *was* open. People came in for their morning coffee and Danish. Some stayed, reading newspapers as they sipped. A few sat outdoors, beneath the awning, despite the cold and damp. The two of you stayed indoors, drinking coffee. There was no real subject for conversation, so you kept quiet, though you were not comfortable with all the mystery and silence.

Then, without preamble, save for a clearing of the throat and a quiet

— So, you know . . .

she launched into a monologue, and followed it with a bizarre proposition. You were young, your surroundings were unfamiliar, and you had expected a flustered confession on the order of "I like to be bound and bitten." Instead, she told you the following:

Years before you met, Mylène Saint-Brieuc had worked in an office in Vannes. The position was beneath her: secretary to an accountant. But her father had insisted she do something that would help her appreciate the lives of those with little money. So, she had allowed herself to become menial. If this was an indignity, there was worse to come. She fell in love with the accountant and they had been having an affair for some time when the accountant's wife got wind of it. *This* was the proper start of her misfortune. The accountant's wife, it was said, was a witch, a real witch: quiet woods, apparitions, toads nailed to trees in a clearing. Mylène believed in none of this, so when the woman came to the office and warned her to leave Vannes, she did not leave. Worse, she carried on her affair with the witch's husband. Two weeks later, though, Mylène fell ill. She could not sleep at night. She was constantly awakened by voices talking about her, her clothes, her behaviour. In the morning, she would feel impure. She couldn't eat and she began to lose weight. Naturally, she went to a doctor. He found nothing wrong. Her family took her to neurologists, to psychologists, all to no avail. Everyone was afraid she would lose her sanity before dying. And then, at last, almost timidly, the accountant visited her home to tell Mylène that his wife, of whom he seemed proud, had in fact cursed her. The witch had put a powder of some sort on Mylène's chair and Mylène had absorbed it over two weeks — a very long time. There was nothing he or anyone could do. She should certainly leave Vannes, however, if she wished to live. And as she wished to live, Mylène quit Vannes the following day, leaving everything behind, moving into an apartment in Neuilly. Did her troubles stop in Neuilly? No, not at all. The voices that had disturbed her sleep grew more distinct. There were now seven of them: men, women, and even a child. Each of them wanted something, each tormented her. None would leave her alone. She was possessed by spirits. In desperation, she went to the church and was seen by priests. It was here, finally, that she found some relief. An exorcist took on her case and chased most of the spirits away . . .

You looked into her eyes, to see if, beneath or beyond the good clothes and personable mien, there was a hint of madness.

— You think I'm lying, she said.

— No, not at all, you answered. It's just I don't know what this has to do with me. Would you like me to wear a soutane when we make love?

She held up her hand and laughed. Then, as if finally remembering that you were indoors, she took off her beret and undid the belt of her raincoat.

— No, no, she said. You've misunderstood. The priest managed to drive out all of the spirits except one. But the one that stayed is the worst. He won't leave because his only desire is to have sex with me.

— Ahh . . . I see.

— No, you don't see. I've tried everything. I've been exorcized by three different priests. I've tried sleeping in a church. Nothing works. I sleep a few hours, here and there, in the day, but at night he comes in and I can't stop him. It's revolting, unbearable. I think he comes because I don't have a man, someone to stay the night with me. But it's impossible for me to find a man with this being around. If I could have *someone* spend the night with me, I'm sure it would drive him away.

— It sounds like a good idea. Why haven't you tried this before?

— I *have* tried it. Often. But no man or woman has managed to stay the night. They've all been frightened away. One of them had a heart attack. I thought I had killed him. I know you don't believe what I'm saying, but it's all true. I haven't had a night's sleep in

64

years. I'm afraid I never will again. You see my predicament?

You must have laughed, though you don't remember laughing. What you do remember is the early morning smell of La Havane, the soap used to clean the zinc, the smell of coffee, the weight of a cube of sugar between your fingers. You also remember Mylène's face: an expression anticipating bad news. She had told this story before, often. In fact, she'd told it so well, you wondered if she believed her own words and then wondered when, during your night together, she would drop the fantasy and become herself: while you were engaged, or afterwards, as she sank into sleep? It didn't matter to you, though, because you found the situation amusing. You were to be paid to spend the night with a woman, not for her pleasure or yours but for the sake of a spirit who wished (as you wished, frankly) to molest her. There was something in her "gentle madness" you found irresistible.

— I'll stay with you, you said, but we'll have to agree on a price. I'll sleep with you for four thousand francs a night.

— I've given you a thousand, she answered. Tomorrow morning I'll give you the rest.

You spent the rest of the day together.

You should remember more than you do, but,

honestly, you were bored. You had no idea the day would be a prelude to anything more interesting than the night. You do remember the house in Neuilly. It was on a side street. Its windows looked out onto a stone-paved courtyard in which, that day, there was a child's tricycle. Or they looked down onto a narrow street, across which was an identical house front. The house had no window curtains and should have been brighter than it was. But it was November. The days were wet and grey and the light was as dull as if it had been passed through a teabag. The furniture, what little there was, was disposed in the centres of the rooms. There were no pieces against the walls. The chairs, lamps, divans, and tables (all brightly painted or brightly upholstered) were in the middle of the rooms. While the middle of her rooms were clean, the edges were dusty and unkempt. Also, the house smelled of almonds, a scent Mylène found soothing. Whenever she was distracted, she would rub almond essence in the wood or on her belongings. This was pleasant, at first, but after a while it was as if the place were made of marzipan and you found the smell cloying.

Mylène bought lunch and a bottle of Pastis, your favourite drink, and you spent the afternoon eating and drinking and talking about your lives. The men and women who wanted you were almost never inter-ested in your biography, but with her you shared any number of details: your parents' hopes for you (Medicine), your dissatisfaction with life in Ottawa, your fondness for raspberries. Neither did she avoid speaking of herself. She told you everything you wanted to know, so that, as evening approached, you were at ease in each other's company. She seemed to you a slightly unfortunate, middle-aged woman (34), too superstitious for her own good.

— Do you believe in God? you asked.

— Of course, she answered.

— Well, that's your problem right there, you said. Atheists aren't bothered by ghosts.

— Don't make fun. Spirits take the bodies they please. I didn't believe in God, until all this started.

As the day waned and it grew colder outside, Mylène turned up the heat. The house was, by late afternoon, so warm you were both sweating. She noticed your discomfort and said, as if in apology

— Neuilly is so cold, it's like a suburb made of marble.

Perhaps the most remarkable thing, when you recall the hours leading to her bed, was the feeling of camaraderie that stole over you. You were not, in those days, as fond of women as you are now, but you felt the stirrings of a sympathy. This was, in part, because you didn't believe a word about her "spirit," and also because you did not believe that her reasons

67

for inventing him could be malicious. You thought: this is some game they play in Neuilly-sur-Seine, in order to have memorable sex.

— What's your spirit's name? you asked.

— Georges, she answered.

And the two of you laughed; you at what you took to be the absurdity of her invention, she at the drabness of her tormentor's name.

There was an awkwardness between you when you finally decided to go to bed. You were at ease, but she became visibly upset at the thought of how you should go about this business. Was it best for "Georges" to find you both naked in bed? One dressed, one naked? Should you make love before the apparition? After? During? (You did not think you could perform for a phantom who was waiting his turn.) Should you make love at all? It might anger "Georges," and then there was no telling what would happen. The thought that you might be hurt, as some of the others had been, seemed to upset her.

— How have you gone about this in the past? you asked.

Oh, she had tried every variation she could think of, writing in a leather-bound diary the procedure she'd followed with each of the men who'd attempted to spend the night. None had lasted the whole night, but each was commemorated by his or her own variation, as you would be whether you lasted the night or not. You lay on the bedsheets, clothed, while Mylène lay naked beneath them.

As with the other rooms, the furniture (the bed, a cabinet) was in the centre of the room. The bedroom, however, was the one room with images hanging on the walls. There were some thirty or forty small crucifixions, thirty or forty reproductions of the *same* painting, hanging on three of the four walls. Above and beneath each reproduction was a tiny, gold crucifix. In the fourth wall was a French window leading out onto a balcony that looked out on the courtyard below.

You were uncomfortable, lying on top of the bedsheets, warm because the heat had been turned up to thirty degrees. You were uncomfortable beside Mylène, who, true to her plans, did not touch you but rather turned away and tried to sleep, although, for some time, you could feel her wakeful presence.

Eventually, slightly annoyed, you fell asleep.

And you woke as a church bell in the distance struck faintly. You began to feel cold. Actually, you must have awakened *before* the bell rang, because you heard each of its eleven clangs, though they were faint. If you had not been awakened by the cold or the bells, you would certainly have been by the sound of Mylène speaking in her sleep. She spoke clearly and slowly, though you've long forgotten her words. When you opened your eyes there was only the darkness and Mylène's voice. And then the cold went straight to your lungs and core. The hair on the back of your head stood up. You felt as if you'd been plunged into ice water and your heart could not take it.

All at once, beside you, beside the bed, looking down at you, was a man, solid as far as you could tell, his eyes wide open, as if in surprise or outrage. Whatever *he* might have felt, you were terrified. You tried to push him away, but as you did your hand passed through his chest and you fell to the bedroom floor. Admit it, *this* is when you thought of abandoning ship, and the fact that Mylène had not lied to you was, strangely, like a betrayal. Why did you not run? You stood up, groped for the light switch against the wall and turned on the light, convinced the light would change things, which it did. It made them more frightening.

The man was not dissolved by light. He now sat on Mylène's side of the bed, looking at you while fondling Mylène, who was still asleep, her mouth open, eyes closed, damp hair covering her face like netting. Now, too, you might have run, but it was at this point that (for no good reason) fear turned to anger in you.

— Leave her alone, you said.

He looked over at you, continued to touch her, and spoke through her. He spoke, you saw his lips move, but every word came from Mylène's mouth, in her voice.

— Fuck off, he said.

But you said you would not. You lay down on the bed and began to touch Mylène yourself: her hair, her breasts.

— Go bother someone else, you said.

Where you got the nerve to say anything of the sort is a mystery. Apart from the occasional moment of madness, you had been a staunch coward all of your young life. At that moment, beside Mylène, you were terrified, but it was as if terror were a drug that hadn't quite taken over, like an anaesthetic that dulls your limbs but leaves the mind clear. You were frightened but lucid, looking dispassionately at the scene. The man sitting on the bed looking at you was tall. He had dark skin. His hair was cut so short you thought him bald, and he was of a much bigger build than you. The only advantage you had over him was life, and you would not have called it an advantage at that moment. Again speaking through Mylène, he said

— The woman is mine. If you don't leave now, I will kill you.

— Go away, you said.

That was the full extent of your eloquence. "Georges" rose and went to the foot of the bed, looking down at you and at Mylène as if he were speechlessly angry. He put his hand out, as if to take hold of you, and you could feel your heart race. But then, suddenly indecisive, "Georges" turned away, walked to the bedroom door, opened it and went out. When he had been gone for what seemed a while, he again spoke through Mylène.

— If you are here tomorrow, he said, you'll regret it.

And with that, night returned to itself, as if it had awakened from a dream. The darkness was only darkness. The heat was again unbearable and Mylène Saint-Brieuc lay beside you sleeping. You lay back on the bed, away from her, but you did not sleep. The incident had taken all of five minutes. It was not eleven fifteen, but you lay awake for the rest of the night, frightened and unsettled.

The following day began at five in the morning, the hour at which Mylène stretched out her body and, seeing you beside her on the bed, sat up.

— You're still here!

You told her everything: what you'd seen and heard, how "Georges" had appeared and spoken through her and threatened you. When you finished, Mylène rose from the bed and tried to hide her tears. She had been moved not by your words but by the sheer fact that you had stayed. The night had been, she said ecstatically, the first of your life together. You were, she said, "married." You mentioned that your marriage was almost certain to be short. Your life was in danger.

— As long as you're here, she answered, Georges

will never be back. I'm sure of it. That was the best sleep I've had in ten years. I can't do enough for you.

What she did, immediately, was go to the cabinet, and from one of its top drawers she took three thousand francs.

— This is for you, she said, though maybe you don't want it anymore?

— You're wrong, you answered. I still need money for Formentera.

She took your hand and kissed your fingers.

— I'll take you to Formentera, she said. You don't have to think about that.

But something in her rapturous tone annoyed you. You had survived a terrifying night, had stayed in the room with a ghost because you had promised you would, but she acted as if you owed her something more. Also, there was the presumption, the conviction that you would welcome her company or that your friend would welcome her to Formentera. (He would not. He despised women.) Perhaps sensing your annoyance, Mylène changed the subject at once. She helped you undress and left you in the bedroom to sleep undisturbed.

Most of that second day is lost to you. You were exhausted, so you slept until afternoon. And when you woke, still alone in the bedroom, daylight slanting in through the French windows, you allowed yourself to admire the drawer full of franc notes. It was all thousand-franc bills, but there were over a hundred of them. You counted them and then stole five thousand francs.

The change in Mylène was the most striking aspect of the day. She began to treat you with familiarity and reverence, touching you as if you were lovers (which you would soon be) but bending to whatever whim you happened to express. And then, too, there was Mylène's body. The heat in the house had been left up, so you sat around without much clothing. Her breasts were fuller than you had imagined when you'd met at Place Winston Churchill. Her skin was pale, as if she hadn't seen the sun for months. The hair on her pudendum was light brown at its edges, dark and untrimmed in the centre. This you particularly remember, because she apologized for it.

Also, there was her look of anguish at the thought that you might not stay a second night. Afraid to insult you by offering money, but knowing that money was among the things you wanted, she said

— I'll give you twice as much if you stay.

Now, as to money: your parents were wealthy. Your father had given you ten thousand dollars for this trip to Europe. He had also warned you not to ask for more. So, yes, the offer of more money was important. At the time, you would have said that money was the *only* thing that kept you. But now? Now you're not sure what was behind your inexplicable bouts of courage. There must have been something deeper than money, something you would have loathed to admit at the time: idealism, maybe, the same instinct that brought revulsion at the thought that your pleasure should supersede hers. Whatever it was, you committed a further act of heroism that bound you to a woman for whom, otherwise, you didn't have strong feelings.

— Yes, okay. I'll stay.

None of this "courage" kept you from terror.

In fact, the second night was worse than the first. On the first night, you'd had no solid reason to believe in "Georges." But on the second, you knew he was actual, whatever he actually was. You and Mylène slept together beneath the sheets of the bed. She laid her arm across your chest and fell asleep facing you. You did not sleep. You waited for eleven o'clock, and heard the bells faintly ring, and then twelve, and then one. The hours of the night passed easily until three in the morning. Then the room grew cold, the hair on your head stood up, and you could feel such malevolence it was as if you were implicated in a terrible crime. Rising from the bed, you got up in time to catch "Georges" beside Mylène, his hand beneath the covers, near her midsection. Seeing you, however, he stood back, closed his eyes, and disappeared. Mylène woke, asked if it were morning, and, on being told it was not, pulled the covers up to her neck, turned away, and fell asleep.

For three more days, this, with slight variations, was how your nights passed. Mylène slept peacefully while you tried to sleep around the visitations: sleep . . . terror . . . sleep.

For years now, you've wondered about two aspects of that November: yourself and Mylène Saint-Brieuc. You're still slightly baffled by your courage but, in a sense, it was a version of your stubbornness, wasn't it? In your twenties, you hated doing whatever was expected of you. The thought that you would run out, as all the others before you had done, must have nettled. You stayed, despite your terror, so that no one could say you had fled. Perhaps this is true, but it is only a guess. At the time, you were in that odd state that characterized your twenties: you knew yourself both well and not at all. You thought about yourself constantly, obsessively, but you could not understand what or who you were. For a while, what you knew best and what you knew least were one and the same.

Mylène, of course, is still a mystery.

In 1980, you were too self-involved to care deeply about anything that didn't involve you directly. You were attentive, but not attentive enough. You thought all of Mylène's behaviour was motivated by her fear of being left with "Georges." But by her own account, she had, when you met, been living with "Georges" for years. She had been in constant search of escape and constant terror of night, it's true, but she must have had strong resources. She had lived a life, before she met you. Her house was itself a testament to that life. No curtains: so there might be light in every room and relief from an interior she found oppressive. Furniture in the centre of a room: to give her things to run behind or around. Almonds: a smell she associated with North Africa, a place she imagined boundless and uninhabited by ghosts. Though she said she had spent years looking for a man like you, she had managed on her own. In fact, she was a much stronger woman than you realized.

The plain fact of your situation struck you, around day four or five, when it occurred to you that the world was contriving to keep you in Neuilly. In the morning, Mylène would bring in an espresso, a croissant still warm from the boulangerie around the corner, and a small pot of the grapefruit marmalade she made herself. The night's sleep having refreshed her — each morning brought her greater and greater well-being — you would go out for walks around Neuilly or take a bus into Paris proper. You spent two whole days in Paris, buying books, eating in well-known restaurants, walking along the Seine, visiting galleries and museums.

You would happily return to those few days in Paris, wouldn't you? And you would find it easy to love the woman who offered them to you. At the time, however, you found all sorts of reasons to be unhappy. You resented it when Mylène refused to buy you a pair of black leather boots you wanted, or when she left too great a tip at Café Flores, or when, as you walked along the riverside, she walked too slowly. Every little thing annoyed you, because you were not her husband and you hadn't chosen this life. Seeing that her behaviour irritated you, Mylène would try to accommodate your moods, walking more quickly, buying anything you happened to glance at. She did everything to put you at ease, though this desire to accommodate was as irritating as anything else. After five days, you could scarcely hide your resentment.

From Mylène's perspective, the thought that the two of you were a bad match must have brought anxiety and distress. She had come to take your presence for granted. Your irritability, the fact that you were not a good match, must have brought her up against the realization that, sooner than she wanted, she would again be alone with "Georges." Being an optimist, she must have assumed there were ways to meet both your needs: hers for company, yours for freedom. But there was not. There never was, was there? In the matter of Formentera, for instance, she again suggested you go together. She would be happy to pay for everything, so long as you could sleep in the same bed. You refused outright, telling her flatly that your friends did not like women and that you would find it awkward to have her with you. Suspecting, then, that you were homosexual and so in need of more "eroticism," she made love to you according to what she imagined your capacity to be. But, being twenty-one, you could barely keep up to yourself sexually and, after a few days of uninhibited lovemaking, she complained she was "uncomfortable." You took this as an insult, and would not speak to her until she apologized.

Finally, when you had been living together for six days and things were at breaking point, she spoke to you simply and honestly, putting aside any desire to please or impress. You were reading when Mylène walked in and sat on the bed beside you.

— We have to talk, she said.

— About what?

— About me, she said.

A subject of no interest to you, but she pleaded for a little of your time. You could not imagine, she said, the life she had been leading for the past five years. Her world had been shattered. None of the wealth or any of the ideas her family had passed on were useful. As far as her family was concerned, there were no ghosts, and it was impossible that she should be assaulted by a man who was not there. So, she had not insisted, preferring to have them think there was something "neurologically" wrong with her. The word "neurology" was as mysterious and sinister to them as "ghost," but by using a medical term she made herself an invalid and avoided an asylum in Bretagne. Agreeing to scientific terminology also meant that she had tacitly agreed to call the real horror she faced (and that you had witnessed) a delusion. So, over the last years, she had made herself as lonely as one could imagine. And then there was "Georges" himself, wasn't there? She could not convey her revulsion at being violated. There wasn't even the possibility of pleasure. "Georges" was not a man but rather a terrifying presence with whom she shared the knowledge of her violation. For years now, she had been unable to sleep at night. Night was for wandering the streets of Neuilly. She slept, if at all, from dawn until mid-afternoon. Yes, naturally, she had tried sleeping with other men, but none had been as faithful as you, none as courageous. They had all fled. This is what made you miraculous: you had remained. You had brought night and sleep back into her life.

She was not blind. She knew the kind of man you were: a thief, at very least.

— I've never stolen anything from you, you said indignantly.

But of course you had, of course. She knew exactly how much money she kept on hand. But . . . but . . . she was *pleased* you'd stolen from her. It meant you might be influenced by money, that you might stay if she gave you more, if she bought things for you. Money meant nothing to her, if it kept you in Neuilly. In fact, she wished you were *more* greedy because, to her disappointment, it was clear money was not enough. She could not hold you with banknotes, nor with her body, nor with desire. She had nothing with which to keep you. So, there you were, then, two human beings, though only one was reduced to raw need. Perhaps, she said, you didn't understand what it meant to have had night restored to her. To her, it was as if she had been returned to life. She would have traded love, money, anything at all for the sleep you'd brought. And so, appealing to your humanity, she asked you to stay, if only for a few more weeks, a month, long enough to give her the strength to go on.

It's shameful to think, isn't it, that this appeal to your humanity was an appeal to something you did not then possess. Indignant (and humiliated) as you were by the mention of your thieving, everything in you rose up against her. You pretended you'd understood her plea, you pretended you'd been moved. You said

— Yes, of course, I'll stay.

though you intended to leave the very next morning. You must have said the words ironically, however, or maybe you put into them a hint of your intentions, because Mylène seemed unconvinced.

— I'm glad you're staying, she said.

You weren't any more convinced by her words than she had been by yours, but you didn't care. You would spend the night. You would leave in the morning. Your only thought was whether you would finish the book you were reading.

— Let me make you some tea, she said.

It was a tisane of some sort, a verveine or vetiver, something herbal enough to overwhelm the medicinal taste of the tablet she must have dissolved in it. You drank the tea and, though it was only mid-afternoon, you fell easily and uncomprehendingly asleep.

You woke up light-headed, unsure where you were, but with a feeling of well-being. For a few moments you couldn't understand why your wrist was sore and then, when you saw that you were handcuffed to the bed, you thought it was some strange (but not unusual) device used in Neuilly to protect one's hands. It did not occur to you that you were being held against your will. Rather, you tried to puzzle out rational reasons for your state: one hand handcuffed to the head of the bed, your feet tied to the bottom. You called out, of course, still bewildered, and Mylène came in.

— What's going on? you asked.

She sat on the bed beside you.

— I'm going to keep you here for a while, she answered. You're going to stay with me for a while. It isn't fair for you to leave. I've only had a week's sleep. I need more.

You looked at her, then, as if meeting her for the first time. Suddenly you were given information that changed everything. Her light brown hair with its wayward *mèche*, her body, her voice, the taut muscles of her arm, her pale skin, her unpainted fingernails . . . everything now pointed to the crucial (and entirely obvious) detail you had missed: as well as being cultured, wealthy, and delicate, Mylène was ruthless. Moreover, she had the means to keep you for as long as she wanted. Another obvious thing: you were nothing to her but a passage to sleep. She had been friendly, because friendliness had been good strategy. She had tried to reason with you, because reason is less trouble than force. All that she had been she had been for convenience' sake, a means of attracting you to her cause. Once you'd stayed the night, you became something else to her: a necessity, at least in her mind, and she would not let you go. Wide awake and fully aware of your situation, you began to call out for help.

— Calm down, she said. I won't let you leave me. You have to accept that.

When you would not calm down, she tied your free hand to the headboard, wound duct tape over your mouth, and sat with you for a while.

Everything changed, the moment she bound you to the bed.

Although, over five nights, your fear of "Georges" had considerably lessened, the night you spent handcuffed and tied to Mylène's bed was and is the worst night you have spent on Earth. It isn't only because of what happened. It is, also, because you discovered your own vulnerability. And something deeper, a frightening thought that came in the middle of the night: what if there were no ghost, no "Georges," but only the projection and will of Mylène herself?

As if in apology, Mylène had made one of your favourite meals: lamb tajine. She fed you herself, then brought you a bedpan. In the interim between being bound to the bed and the approach of evening, you had decided you would not give Mylène the satisfaction of hearing you plead or ask for anything. So, you refused to speak to her, eating because you were hungry and then turning away. Your silence did not disturb her at all, though. She again put tape over your mouth to keep you from calling out in the evening.

—Goodnight, she said. I'm sorry to do this, but at least you won't have to suffer as long as I have.

Meaning: she would release you eventually?

Meaning: she was no monster, whatever you happened to think of her in this, the time of her distress?

At the thought that you were defenceless, that you could not even run from the room, you grew too distraught to sleep. You waited. The night was bright. The moon shone on the world, turning everything white, including the rectangles of light that passed through the French doors and illuminated your side of the bedroom. As the hours passed, the moonlight grew brighter and brighter until, at one in the morning, it would have been difficult to fall asleep, frightened or not.

Then, as the distant bells began ringing for two, "Georges" entered the room.

On this night, he came first to your side of the bed and looked down at you, his mouth open so you could see he had two teeth missing. Though the moonlight was behind him, you could see him clearly: a tall man with broad shoulders and a long neck, his ears as if pressed to his skull. He looked down at you, smiled maliciously, and touched your chest, a sensation you have often compared to swallowing a cold, partially deflated balloon: suffocating and vile. You would have said or done anything to stop him. But as it happened, he was not interested in you. He was simply pleased to see you bound and out of the way. He withdrew from the moonlight and went to Mylène's side of the bed.

You did not see what followed. You heard it, rather, and felt it. First, there was his voice through hers: a kind of low rumbling. Then, as if a man had truly climbed onto the bed with you, the mattress sank under his weight and he began to fuck her. The noise of their fucking — his sighs and groans, her groans and cries of awareness and distress — was all in her voice, and it is the most disturbing thing you have heard: two beings using the same voice, almost simultaneously. And every nuance was conveyed, from "Georges'" pleasure to Mylène's growing disgust and resistance. The whole of it lasted some fifteen minutes before you felt "Georges" rise from the bed. He came into the moonlight to look at you and smile, and then he was gone.

You felt, as "Georges" left the bedroom, that you would rather die than go through an episode like the one you had just survived. But if you were disgusted and afraid, it was obviously worse for Mylène. She was quiet for some time, but you could feel her body shaking on her side of the bed. Then it was as if a banshee had entered the room. Mylène let out a cry of grief and outrage that was itself as frightening as "Georges" had been. Jumping up from bed, she ran from the room, talking to herself and shouting words in your direction.

It was frightening, but it was also, strangely amusing: one hand cuffed to a bed, the other tied to the headboard, feet tied to the footboard, at the mercy of a woman who seemed to be mindlessly rushing about a house in Neuilly. You, of course, couldn't speak, your mouth having been taped shut. Yes, it was, in its bewildering illogic, amusing. And you were helplessly amused even when Mylène returned to the room with a broom and began to strike you with its handle. Now, this changed your mind for you. She broke two of your fingers and hurt your ribs so that it was weeks before you could breathe without pain. Her frenzy, as she hit you, was indescribable, and it was not clear that she would stop.

But stop she did. When she had exhausted herself, Mylène dropped the broom and turned on the bedroom lights. Then, as if the light brought remorse, she began to cry. And this, oddly, was one of the more disturbing moments in an evening filled with them. Disturbing to *you* because, as Mylène sat on the bed crying, it finally occurred to you that you were in a world whose prelate was the woman who'd just beaten you with a broom handle. Save for you yourself, what in this compact universe was *not* of her making? "Georges," the smell of almonds, the pictures and crucifixes? You were at the mercy of an unknowable and strange woman who might, on a whim, punish you as she was punishing herself.

When she could speak without sobbing, Mylène repeated the same question over and over, as much to herself as to you:

— Why didn't you protect me? Why didn't you protect me?
until, as the bells faintly struck three, the question
exhausted itself as had her rage and she sat silently
awake staring at the wall.

The following day, as she bandaged your broken fingers to a splint, you spoke together with surprisingly
little rancour, bound by your shared experience of
her demons and by a mutual fear, each of the other.
Ashamed of herself, she had agreed to let you go, but
only when she was certain you would not hurt her for
what she had done. While you, naturally, found her
unnerving and thought only of leaving.

— I've never done anything like this before, she
said. I've never hurt anyone.

You assured her that you believed every word, but
you could not stay. And it was thoroughly understood
by both of you that, for whatever reason, you could not
be held against your will and still defend her against
"Georges." Thank Christ for that. You were free to go
and that is what you wanted, and yet, as you watched
her bind your fingers to the splint, you were almost
overwhelmed by pity.

Mylène Saint-Brieuc did nothing to elicit pity or
any other emotion. Her hair held back by barrettes, she
sat beside you on the bed, your hand in her hands as if

it were a wounded bird. You watched as she carefully wound the bandage, pulling it taut around the splint, the ring finger, and the baby finger of your left hand. The white cloth, the clumsy scissors with the fading word "Singers" embossed on one of its blades, and the silver fasteners which she used to keep the bandage in place: like little insects, smooth figure eights on one side, with what looked like tiny, triangular teeth on the other.

She did not look at you as she bound your fingers. Embarrassed, humiliated, it's likely she wanted you gone as much as you wanted to go. Now that you could not help her, what could your presence bring except further humiliation? It would have brought little consolation that you were the only other being on Earth who knew of what her nights consisted. When she had finished and there was nothing more to say, you got up to leave. She gave you twenty thousand francs for Formentera. She held the door open for you to leave.

— Forgive me, she said
looking down at the floor, no doubt already steeling herself against the visitations to come.

And you would have left without a word, were it not for the onset of a question: as she held the door open for you, as you passed beneath the lintel, you wondered if you had the right to leave, knowing exactly what she would face when or if she fell asleep.

— I'll give you five days, you said. I'll stay for five nights. I can't leave you like this.

And in that moment, briefly, you thought you knew what it meant to be human. And you have never forgotten the feeling, though, of course, you were wrong. Looking up at you in alarm, Mylène said

— I don't want you here

and closed the door in your face.

The rest of your time in Europe was insignificant, or insignificant for you.

You did not go to Formentera. As you were on a train to Pamplona, you cracked your arm deflecting a suitcase that fell. A ridiculous, dispiriting accident. You might have spent time in Pamplona, but you were suddenly weary of travel. You returned to Paris, in the hope it would renew your spirits. But after only a day in Barbès, you gave up and went home.

Time passed.

And more time passed.

When you first returned from Europe, you were happy to tell your "ghost story." Your moments of terror and revulsion were a source of amusement to dinner guests. Though few believed the particulars of your tale, the idea of your inconvenient courage was admired. In your telling, you were not kind to Mylène. In your telling, she was a needy harridan, so your escape from her was as admired as your courage in the room with "Georges." For years, whenever a conversation turned to the supernatural you would be asked to recount your time with Mylène. Certain details were fixed in memory and in storytelling: the smell of almonds, furniture in the centre of a room, paintings and crucifixes nailed to a wall.

But after the death of your wife, you never told your "ghost story" again.

Still more time passed . . .

Work was the principal thing that freed you from loneliness and longing: work and travel. Over the years, you visited England, Africa, Thailand, Australia. You travelled on a whim or on business. But you visited Europe no more than two or three times, to see Budapest, Munich, Luxembourg. Nor did you think of Mylène all that often. You had managed to put that "strange dream" behind you. Until, finally, wishing to see Paris again, you returned to the city in late summer so you could have the streets "to yourself."

And one afternoon, as you were walking along the Seine, it began to rain and you went into the Bistro Matin Doré. It looked a little down at the heels from the outside, and that suited you fine. Over the years, you had developed a tolerance for places where the food is indigestible, the wine has an aftertaste of chalk, and the lighting is carnivalesque. You do not seek these places out, but the life within them interests you. So, you were slightly disappointed when, on entering, you saw that the Matin Doré was elegant, well lit but intimate, a bistro of exceptional quality.

You sat in a booth, ordered a *confit de canard* and a red wine from Cahors, and stared mindlessly out at the falling rain.

— Excuse me, but I believe we know each other.

Beside you, suddenly, was an elegantly dressed woman in her sixties or seventies. Her hair was grey, recently permed so that it looked as if she had just gotten out of bed. She was slim and self-assured. There *was* something familiar about her, but not enough, until she said

— Your name is Robert, isn't it? You see? *I* have not forgotten *you*.

Your name has never been Robert, but the woman's smile was mischievous, and it was by this that you recognized Mireille. The odd thing is that, although she knew your face, she did not know who you were. That is, she knew you had been intimate, but she almost certainly had you confused with another of her lovers, one with whom she'd had a memorable affair. Yours had not been memorable, save for her having given you the telephone number of her cousin, Mylène. Still, you stood up, kissed her hand, and invited her to share the booth with you.

— You don't mind being seen with such an old woman?

— You look so much younger than I, you said. I should be asking you the question.

She smiled again.

— You're a vile flatterer, she said. But I'll stay for a tisane. I have to meet my husband in half an hour. It's hard to believe he's still alive, isn't it? Sometimes I think he holds on just to give me something to complain about. Oh, I love him, certainly I love him, but the way one loves a cat, you see? I wouldn't like to see him run over by a car, but when his time comes I'll be grateful for the peace and quiet.

— A successful marriage? you asked.

— The most successful. I'm quite proud of my marriage but, after a while, it has a life of its own, not so? I hear news of it at times like this when I have to meet my husband. But tell me about yourself. Did you ever marry your Polish countess?

You considered telling her who you actually were: a man with whom she had spent a few days thirty years previously, indulging her erotic whims. You did not, because she would almost certainly have been embarrassed, given the reality of your affair. And then there was the matter of Mylène. You wanted to know what had happened to her, and you weren't sure Mireille would tell you if she were reminded that you were a man who had stolen from her. So, you lied about the countess (with whom you said you had had two children) and then gently you brought the conversation around to Mylène.

— Who? Mylène? How do you know my cousin?

— You told me about her, you answered.

Mireille frowned, and you were afraid you had pushed your luck. But before you could change the subject or, at least, suggest you leave it alone, she said

— Mylène was always such a fantasist. She had the strangest ideas. She thought she was possessed by spirits. Did I tell you that?

— No, not at all. Look, if the subject is unpleasant . . .

— It's not unpleasant, my dear little Myshkin. In fact, it's amusing. A long time ago, when my husband and I lived in Montmartre, Mylène moved into a house in Neuilly. My aunt asked me to look out for her, but Mylène was always a little . . . uncanny. Frankly, I couldn't stand her for more than an hour. The hair on the back of my neck would stand up. I made sure she had what she needed. You're going to think I'm very rude, but I used to send her men, so she wouldn't be too lonely. Then one day, without the least warning, she left Neuilly and went to Formentera. Why? Because she was obsessed with one of the stupid little gigolos I'd sent over. Can you imagine?

— Well, that's a reason, you said.

—Yes, if the man she was after had *been* on Formentera. But he hadn't. Seems she never saw him again, but she stayed all the same. Honestly, it broke my poor aunt's heart. And do you know, Mylène has never come home, not even for her parents' funeral. And do you know why? Because she can sleep through the night on Formentera. And why is that? Because she's convinced the spirits that used to haunt her cannot travel over water. Have you ever heard anything so ridiculous?

Mireille laughed.

—Oh, the power of the human mind, she said. First she believes she's possessed, and then because some medium tells her that spirits can't travel over water, she believes she is free. I'll tell you something, my dear Myshkin, I myself have never valued sleep so much that I'd live on Formentera for it. She has her parents' fortune. She does nothing but dabble in watercolours and walk around the island. It's all she's done for years and years! But this is all quite absurd. Let's talk about something else. I seem to remember you were easily aroused, in the old days. Is this still true? Now that I'm an old woman, you can tell me these things quite openly, you know?

You spoke on for a while as she drank her tisane and then, true to her word, she went off to meet her husband, leaving you with her card and an invitation to lunch the following day. You finished your duck and your wine, by which time it had stopped raining and the sky above the city was visible through the clouds.

As you walked along the wet streets towards your hotel, you thought of going to Formentera yourself, of searching for Mylène as she must once have searched for you. Of course, Mylène would not have looked for you out of any kind of love. If she had looked for *you* at all, it would have been out of desperation, a final hope for sleep. But why should you look for her, an old woman who had found peace? Why should you seek *her* out? What would you say if you found her?

— I am sorry for this. I am sorry for that. You have taught me something valuable, though I can't quite name it . . .

And, in fact, what had your short time together brought you? Shame, terror, the first inklings of the other world, of death, and an unguarded moment: Mylène tending to your broken fingers. What had your time together brought her? Formentera. An expensive prison, and sleep. Well, that was something, wasn't it? Yes, but in the end, you had no desire to cross the seas and carry the past back to her. You would only have reminded her of terrible things. Your coming would have meant "Georges."

So, as you walked to your hotel, you were easily reconciled to the thought that you and Mylène Saint-Brieuc would not see each other again. Not in this world.

KAWABATA

In late April, Bernard Crowe volunteered to lead a few men north to survey the brush around Nagagami Lake. He left for Hornepayne days before the others, to see about lodgings and transportation. Years had passed since his wife's death, but the need for solitude, a need that had come with her funeral, sometimes overtook him and he often travelled to be alone.

On his first day in Hornepayne, he woke early and walked about the town's black-snow-gritted streets. He took the Lake Road halfway to the lake and then back. The walk was exactly what he'd wanted: bracing, the sun coming up to brighten the rocks and trees. There was more snow than he'd expected, snow coarse as rock salt, white beneath the trees but dark closer to the road. The trees were dense and green or black and skeletal. He walked on grass that had survived the winter — or had not survived but stood up anyway.

On his return to the bed and breakfast where he'd rented a room, he was met by his hostess, Mrs. Vetiver, a large woman, her hair fixed so it was like a dun hat with grey threads. She wore a white pinafore with red and yellow sunflowers over a blue summer dress.

— Oh, Mr. Crowe, she said. I've made grits with maple syrup and back bacon. There's freshly squeezed melon juice and a blackberry compote. I hope you like it.

— I'm sure it'll be great, he answered. Thank you.

For the rest of the day, Bernard did little. He made certain that reservations had been made at the hotel for himself and his crew. He walked about Hornepayne, quietly pacing its dozen or so streets, and he was charmed by a snowfall, flakes wispy as dandelion fluff, melting as they touched his skin. The town was modest and plain, but as all places are beautiful immediately after a harsh winter, it was also beautiful.

At supper that evening, there were three people: Bernard himself, Mrs. Vetiver, and a pale woman, her brown hair held up by a black band, the down along her neck translucent.

— Mr. Crowe, said Mrs. Vetiver, this is Mrs. Andrews. She'll be with us a few days. Almost as long as you, now I think of it.

Bernard, who had taken the chair beside Mrs. Andrews, said

— Pleased to meet you.

Mrs. Andrews raised her head, turned towards him, and smiled politely. Three deliberate motions. Her eyes were lovely, though it was as if she had been crying or had recently awakened.

— Nice to meet you, she said.

They ate their meal in a quiet broken only by Mrs. Vetiver's commentary on the day she'd had and the dishes she had prepared. Once they'd eaten and had coffee, Mrs. Andrews rose and, taking Bernard's hand, wished him a good night's sleep.

— Thank you, said Bernard.

He would have said more, but Mrs. Andrews looked away and left the dining room. Mrs. Vetiver insisted on clearing the table herself, so Bernard went to his room, climbed up the stairs thinking of Mrs. Andrews's eyes. They were somehow familiar: blue-green with long, light lashes.

Bernard's room had once been a playroom. Its walls were robin's-egg blue, with a gold band running above the quarter-round. His bed was good, not too soft, and there was a large window that looked out on a rise in the land, beyond which was the rough, darkening forest. He was not tired, but he felt a kind of peace, a near absence of longing. For a few hours, he tried to read a book someone had recommended, then fell asleep without turning off the light on his night table.

The next morning, as he went out for a walk, Bernard saw Mrs. Andrews on the street before him. Quickening his pace, he caught up and they walked together. Mrs. Andrews was as reserved as she'd been the night before. They exchanged few words until they turned back to Mrs. Vetiver's and Bernard asked if she (Clara Andrews) was in Hornepayne on business. After a moment, Mrs. Andrews said

— Yes. And you?

— Yes, me too. I work for the federal government.

— You must be from Ottawa, she said. My father was from Ottawa.

For the next while, Mrs. Andrews kept to those subjects (her father and Ottawa), deflecting questions that might lead elsewhere. Bernard did not mind, because it had been two years, two years almost exactly, since he'd had anything like an intimate conversation with a woman. Still, there was something forbidding about her choice of subjects and, after a while, his mind wandered and he looked up at the morning sky, which was grey, though here and there the sun came through, illuminating patches of town and forest.

As they approached the bed and breakfast, Mrs. Andrews suddenly stopped speaking. Contrite, she said

— I'm so sorry. I've been going on and on.

But before Bernard could demur, she asked

— Are you working today? Maybe we could explore the town together.

It was Saturday. He had nothing in particular to do, but as for exploring the town — that would take little more than an hour, an hour if they went slowly. No matter. He agreed to "do Hornepayne" with her. He went upstairs to bathe and shave. When he came down half an hour later, Mrs. Andrews was on the phone in the front hall.

— I changed my mind, that's all . . . I don't care.

She saw Bernard, turned away, and spoke more softly before hanging up. When she turned back to him, her smile was grim.

Mrs. Andrews was not interested in the town. They went first to the statue of the bear and cub, wandered along a few of the side streets, and then walked to Hornepayne Cemetery. She asked him about himself, but now it was Bernard's turn to be evasive. He spoke of his life in the most fleeting way. And by the time they arrived at the cemetery, they had fallen back into silence.

The sign above the cemetery was like that above a corral: a double arc in which the words HORNEPAYNE and CEMETERY nested, looking very much like a stencil. The white crosses and tombstones were not in strict rows, but there was order. Behind the cemetery, the trees of the woods stood shoulder to shoulder, but they were thin and bedraggled.

— This is the first week they could dig graves, said Mrs. Andrews. The ground's too hard in winter.

— Oh, are you from around here? Bernard asked.

— No, she answered.

Mrs. Andrews lowered her head, and her shoulders began to shake. Bernard thought she had begun to cry but she was laughing.

— What is it? he asked.

— Nothing. I'm in a cemetery in a horrible town with a man I don't know. It feels like I'm dreaming. But I'm glad you're here. Do you mind if I hold your arm?

Bernard gave her his arm, and they went slowly back to the town centre. A small wind ruffled the trees and brought pieces of paper to life. The weight of Mrs. Andrews' arm in his was both comforting and a source of distress, the distress one feels on being handed something fragile. It was almost a relief when they came to the coffee shop and stopped for tea.

The shop was small and a little grimy, but as if this were the place and moment she'd been waiting for, Mrs Andrews began to confide in him, sharing the details of her life. She was in town for her father's death. His funeral was for the next day. She was not sure she should have come. She had never liked her father, had felt nothing for him but disgust since she was six years old. She did not say what, exactly, had disgusted her, but for an hour her world (like a planet) came darkly into view as she sat before him. Bernard studied Mrs. Andrews's face. It was, even when she was distraught or confused, appealing.

As they returned to the bed and breakfast, Mrs. Andrews again took Bernard's arm.

— You've been very kind, she said. I don't know how to thank you, but I wonder if . . . I shouldn't ask, I know, but I don't think I can go to my father's funeral alone. Would you come with me? Please. I don't have anyone else to ask.

He would have preferred to avoid people, and the last thing he wanted was to attend a funeral. But it was not in his nature to turn away from those in distress.

— Yes, of course, he said.

The following day, Bernard went with Clara to her father's funeral. The sky was bright blue. No clouds, little wind, a stillness that penetrated so deeply it was almost odd to find other people in the church. There were not many. There were a handful on one side of the aisle and a smaller handful on the other, all of them near the front. The stained-glass windows on one side of the church were sun-touched and brightly coloured, but their illumination did not reach the centre of the church, which was in mottled shadow. Clara and Bernard were to the right of the altar, three rows back. In the row before them, alone, was Clara's sister. In the row before that, Clara's mother sat. On the other side of the aisle were darkly dressed aunts and uncles. In all, eight people had come to the funeral.

The coffin was in the aisle not far from the altar.

Before they entered the church, Clara had spoken to no one. Nor did anyone seem interested in speaking to her. Clara had entered briskly, as if there for some other business. She had told him the names of those in the church, speaking her mother's and her sister's names with a contemptuous whisper. Hearing Clara's voice, her sister turned around, stared at Bernard for a moment, then turned away.

The priest began the service. There were two altar boys with him, genuflecting, rising, kneeling, bowing awkwardly, out of sync. Their faces were pale. When it was time for the eulogies, the priest said a few words about Mr. Johnson's life — hockey, broken knees, devotion to his lovely daughters, amen — and then Mrs. Johnson spoke of him — hard life, bad knees, love for his daughters, amen. Mrs. Johnson spoke clearly, but her emotions were not clear and there was a hint of defiance in her attitude. She held herself straight, as if expecting a challenge to her words. At the end of her mother's eulogy, Clara nudged Bernard's arm and, having his attention, rolled her eyes and shook her head.

When the mourners had knelt a final time and wished godspeed to the soul of the dead, six young men entered from the sacristy and took up the coffin. They were not as awkward as the altar boys had been. They were freshly scrubbed. The hair on the tallest of them looked pasted to his forehead. Everyone followed the young men out. They watched as the coffin was put into the hearse and the doors closed. In the brief lull after the hearse's departure, Clara's mother spoke to her.

— Where's your husband? she asked.

— He couldn't make it, said Clara.

— Well, it was nice that you and your friend here could come to your father's funeral. Too bad your husband couldn't make it.

One of Clara's aunts approached. She was in a violet pantsuit and wore a dark, black lace veiled hat. Brushing at her clothes as if there were crumbs on her chest, she looked mistrustfully at Bernard.

— Who's this? she asked.

— None of your business, answered Clara.

— Well, for God's sake, Clara. Can't you keep a civilized tongue?

— You know how she is, said Clara's mother. She's had such a *difficult* life, she doesn't remember how to be polite.

— That's right, said Clara.

Turning her back on her daughter, Clara's mother said

— What's wrong with you, Belle? You get dirt on your clothes or you just rubbing your tits?

— No, no, said Belle. Arty fell asleep on me in there. I got his hair all over me. When he goes on night shift, he falls asleep all over the place. Honestly, it's like having one of those long-haired dogs around the house.

They walked away from Clara, to stand with the rest of the family at the foot of the church's steps. No one else expressed any interest in Bernard. No one spoke to Clara. The family stood by the church to shake the priest's hand or, as one did, to clap him on the back. Then they left for the cemetery.

Clara walked away from the church.

— You've been really kind, she said. I wish we could have met in different circumstances.

— Aren't you going to the cemetery?

— No. I've done enough. My husband thought it'd be good to make peace with my father, but I shouldn't have come.

At the door to the bed and breakfast, Mrs. Andrews turned and said

— Thanks again.

Her face was expressionless and she did not wait for Bernard's response. As if she were embarrassed about something, she climbed the stairs and left him in the entrance hall. It was a moment before he came back to himself and then, bewildered, he returned to the outside world. The sunlight was only occasionally impeded by clouds, shadows moving briskly over the face of the earth, and it was warm enough to leave his overcoat unbuttoned.

Bernard walked without a destination, trying to tire himself out. As he came to the centre of town for the third time, he recognized Clara's mother. She was beside a lemon yellow car. She wore the same clothes she'd worn to the funeral: all dark. Seeing him, she stood up straight. Her face was heavily made up, pink-ish, powder-scored, and, as the sun was behind her, in shadow. Her eyes reminded Bernard of her daughter's. Her lips were flat and fire red.

— My husband was a good man, she said. I don't know what Clara told you, but her head's been filled with nonsense since she went to Toronto. Everything's memory this and memory that. Clara's always going on about it. But the way I see it, the past is for people who don't have better things to worry about. That's just the way I see it.

Bernard said

— Well, yes . . .

but Mrs. Johnson turned, locked the door to her car, and walked away. She did not wait for him to finish speaking.

That evening, Bernard and Mrs. Vetiver were alone in the dining room. The bed and breakfast was almost empty. Mrs. Vetiver had prepared pork hocks in a cranberry reduction, sweet potatoes mashed with a rosemary-infused olive oil, and drunken chocolate cake for dessert.

— Did you like it? she asked when they had finished.

Though it had been an unexpected confluence of flavours, he said

— Yes.

— Why don't you stay another night, then? I'll make coquille Saint-Jacques.

— I wish I could, but I've got to be at the hotel with my crew. We start work tomorrow.

Bernard helped her with the dishes, and wished her goodnight.

Outside his window, the last rays of sunlight turned the sky a reddish blue and made the trees appear darker than they were. He stood before the window thinking of nothing. And then, apropos of nothing, he thought of the funeral. Its details came to him: the church windows, the faces of the mourners, their dark clothes, the smell of candles and pews, the priest's long fingers. How odd it all had been: subdued, and difficult to read. It had been unlike any funeral he'd attended and yet, standing alone in the room that had once held

Mrs. Vetiver's children, staring out at the northern sky which slowly brought forth the moon and the evening star, he was suddenly at another funeral, Elizabeth's: the tall-ceilinged church, the dark panels of the stations of the cross, the sound of a breath caught and held, his mother-in-law, her rosary wrapped so tightly around her hand he thought its beads would fly off, the grief of some sixty people, their emotions deep and unmistakable.

Two more unlike versions of a sacrament one could not have imagined. At the memory of Elizabeth's funeral, sadness rose up and overwhelmed him. Whatever Clara's father had been, however monstrous or kind, his funeral was erased by Elizabeth's. In fact, all funerals were one to Bernard, still all one: they were all Elizabeth's. The past was not a luxury, nor a shadow, nor even a black star.

And yet his grief passed after a moment. After a moment, he returned to himself, as a bank of clouds moved between the moon and the tops of the night-blackened trees. He was alone and in the dark, but his thoughts were not about darkness or solitude. He thought about Clara and her mother. He wondered if he was as mysterious to them as they were to him, wondered if the living are more mysterious than the dead, wondered, finally, if the dead are as restless as the living.

Then, as happened only rarely now, a moment from his life with Elizabeth surfaced, whole but brief: beads of water on her neck and shoulder blades, as he moved a bar of soap (a white eraser) across her white back. Where was she, he wondered, and could she still feel what he felt for her? He sincerely hoped not, hoped she was untroubled. He hoped the chaos of this world was a screen between here and the hereafter.

And with these small hopes in mind, he turned on the bedside lamp and, almost as a matter of course, sought refuge in a book that brought, eventually, only sleep.

PART TWO: RECONCILIATIONS

IVAN ILYCH: A TRAVELOGUE

Anyway . . . yesterday, we saw a big hawk devouring what looked like a bluebird in our backyard, under the lilac tree. This went on for about an hour, until Kim could hold off no longer, and started shovelling snow, at which point the hawk listened carefully for about ten minutes, then took off with what was left of its prey.
— Roo Borson (January 7, 2009)

When we were in Trinidad recently, my mother left a hambone out on the kitchen counter. The hambone was covered in tinfoil, waiting to be boiled with split peas, dumplings, cassava, and onions: split pea soup. It was Christmas, so we'd all eaten more ham than usual. I felt like I'd eaten a pig's hindquarters all by myself. As no one was really interested in the ham, we were less vigilant than we should have been. The hambone was left out for two days.

You can't leave food out for that long, in 30-degree weather. But I was still surprised when I lifted the foil and found a clump of maggots, the size of my fist, writhing over one end of the hambone. Suppressing my disgust, I threw the ham and its hosts out, cleaned the counter with boiling water, and reminded my mother to be more careful, though she was the one who'd warned me, on our first day in Petit Valley, to keep the kitchen clean lest we be overrun by maggots.

It isn't as if, as a Canadian,[3] I don't know about flies and rot. It's just that, on that score, Ontario's climate is slightly more forgiving in summer, and much more so in winter. It takes food less time to rot in warm places. And, in fact, that's one of the ways I know I am in Trinidad, and not at home.

Emotionally, however, things aren't quite so neat. Rot and maggots bring death immediately to my mind, but I first learned about death as a child in Trinidad,

3   I was born in a nursing home in St. Ann's, Trinidad, in 1957. I moved to Canada in 1961. On my return to Trinidad, in 2009, I became aware of an inexistent "André Alexis," one who had not left Trinidad, had not abandoned his extended family or the ground that had given birth to him. I became most vividly aware of this other André Alexis when, in a public washroom in a shopping mall, a man asked me if I were from Belmont. I answered that my *father* was from Belmont but that I had been born in St. Ann's. He told me how much I looked like someone from Belmont and he wanted to discuss my origins. I cut the conversation short and left the washroom feeling how curious it was that someone trying to pick me up should know this thing about my origins simply by looking at my face — a face I have, after all, seen often in mirrors. He could place me in the neighbourhood where my father was born.

and I've never managed to shake the feeling that death itself is Trinidadian.

CRO

A man is walking alone down a narrow lane. It's late at night, quiet and dark. No street lamps, only the moon and stars for light. But the lanes are so familiar that the man could find his way home blindfolded or blind drunk. A breeze blows through San Juan. From time to time, the moon is lost in the folds of a long, fat cloud, but otherwise the night is starlit and bright. Then someone is walking towards him. A woman. He has lived in San Juan all his life, but he doesn't recognize her. She has on a lovely hat that half hides her face. And she is beautiful. In fact, he is so struck by her beauty that when they pass each other he's too flustered to say a word. He simply bows and walks on, wondering where she lives and if he will see her again. Half a mile farther along, another woman approaches. Feeling he'd been impolite to the first one who passed, he is about to greet this second woman when he sees it is the *same* woman. This time, when they pass, he's not flustered. He's frightened. He lowers his head and walks faster. A quarter of a mile farther on, he sees the same woman again. He recognizes her at once and looks down and sees that she has one normal foot and one cloven foot, like a goat. And he is terrified.

He understands that this is La Diablesse and he runs for all he's worth. He can't hear anything, save his own footfalls, but he can feel her behind him, there, keeping up, getting closer and closer. Now he's running for his life. His heart is pounding. His ribs ache. His house is only 50 yards away, but it takes every shred of will to reach it, to open the gate and slam it behind him, to run to his own door. Turning around, he sees La Diablesse on the other side of the gate, her white face like a block of moonlight carved into a mask of frustration and rage.

.— Is a good t'ing yuh ain' say a word, yuh heah?

And with that mysterious, disdainful sentence, she vanishes.

— But what would have happened if he'd said anything? (is what I *always* asked.)

— La Diablesse would have carried his soul away. (The usual answer.)

Not a helpful answer. I had no idea what a "soul" was when I first heard these stories. Nor could anyone really enlighten me. So, for the longest time, "soul" was one of those words that hid more than it revealed. Death is what I imagined when I heard the word "soul," in this case death by a mysterious but beautiful woman. In fact, it was always said that La Diablesse was beautiful, but beautiful only to men. Her beauty had no effect on women, and she wore a hat for the same reason she wore long, elegant skirts: to hide something. The skirts were to hide her cloven hoof, the hat to hide a white, cadaverous face. This beauty — to men (who, by this folk reasoning, are attracted to death) — seemed an unavoidable aspect of La Diablesse, a way to know she was wicked, and my younger self always assumed that a dark-night encounter with a *plain* woman was perfectly acceptable.

Equally fascinating were stories about *Dwens*:

— You know, Mrs. So-and-So was minding her two children, a boy and a girl. The children were in the yard playing when the boy fell and cut himself. The child made so much noise, she took him inside to fix his cuts and bruises. She left the girl alone in the yard, playing. It was late in the day, but it wasn't dark and she wasn't gone long. It was only a minute. But when she came back outside she couldn't find her daughter at all. She called the neighbours. They searched all over the neighbourhood, but the child was gone. Well, you can imagine her distress. But this woman turned out to be one of the lucky ones. Towards evening, her next-door neighbour, who worked in San Juan, brought her child home to her. How did he manage to find the child? Pure chance. That day, the weather was good and he had decided to walk home. He was walking by the river when he saw two children in front of him. Nothing unusual about that, but for some reason, he was looking down in the sand and he noticed two sets of footprints: one set going forward, the other set going backwards. And yet: both children were walking forward. It made no sense. He called out to the children and they both looked back at him. When they turned around, he recognized his neighbour's child, but the other child, the one that had the footprints back to front, had no face.

—No face? How could it have no face?

—It had no eyes, no mouth, no nose, nothing. And the child vanished as soon as the man saw it. And as soon as it vanished? It was like the woman's child came out of a trance and started to cry. You see what I'm telling you? If you hear some child call your name, make sure you look down to see if its feet are turned right way around. If the feet are back to front? That is a *Dwen*.

—What's a *Dwen*?

—A *Dwen* is a child who died before it was baptized. It has no face. Its feet are backwards, and it leads children into the forest to get lost and die or into the river, where they drown. It's only children they want to play with. But sometimes at night, you can hear the *Dwens* crying. It's most annoying.

And then there were stories about *Soucouyants*. A *Soucouyant* is an old woman who can change shape. At night, she sheds her human skin and travels about — often as a ball of fire — turning people into animals or sucking their blood. (There is a great calypso called "Suck meh, *Soucouyant*" about a man who leaves his windows open at night so the *Soucouyant* can fly in and, well, suck his blood.) The thing is, the *Soucouyant* has to get back into her human skin before the cock crows. It's her weakness. If you want to kill a *Soucouyant*, you have to put salt in her skin so that it will shrivel and wither. When the *Soucouyant* then tries to put her skin back on, she is unable to and so she dies. There are other interesting details about *Soucouyants*. For instance, should you want to know if there's a *Soucouyant* in your neighbourhood, all you have to do is go to a crossroads and dump out 100 pounds of rice. The *Soucouyant* — an old woman by day — will be compelled to pick up all the rice one grain at a time. She may be the only obsessive-compulsive evil creature known to man[4] or, perhaps, the most monstrously frugal.

The fact that the *Soucouyant* is obsessive-compulsive is interesting, but the detail, in stories about *Soucouyants*, that puzzles and fascinates me is this: if you manage to put salt in her skin, the *Soucouyant*, before she dies, will cry out over and over

---

4   In some versions, it's said the *Soucouyant* must also *count* each grain as she picks them up.

— 'Kin, 'kin yuh nah know me? 'Kin yuh nah know me?

(Or, to translate: "Skin, skin don't you know me?") imploring her skin to recognize her and to let her back in. This is the thing I can't stop thinking about when I think about *Soucouyants*: a creature pleading with her now-estranged, salt-infested skin. There is, despite the grotesquery, something touching in this. Why? Why should a story of evil include such a pathetic moment, a moment in which one — if one is like me — feels for the evil creature? Why should this detail be so important?

I can think of a number of answers to that question:

1. As they knew in the eighteenth century, the sublime and the grotesque are inextricable, and the moment of identification with the *Soucouyant* is sublime.
2. I am an immigrant. Symbolically, my original skin no longer fits.

   (In which case, I am myself a kind of *Soucouyant*...)
3. Touching details of this sort are precisely what keep a story (or warning) in mind.

Any of those answers would be good fodder for an essay, but I'm interested in the *feeling* those stories instilled in me, in the force of the details: the tears of the *Dwens*, the pleading of the *Soucouyant*, the white face of La Diablesse. I remember an intense pleasure in hearing those stories, but at the same time, I had a near obsessive need to hear them over and over again, because the stories created an unbearable tension that could be relieved only by hearing them. It was as if stories about La Diablesse, *Dwens*, and *Soucouyants* came ever so close to revealing something essential, something you couldn't quite catch but needed to. I listened to these stories until the (adult) storytellers grew bored or tired, but their secret meaning, if there was *a* meaning, always eluded me. The "something" they contain that holds you and eludes you at the same time is, I think, death — the idea of it, the sense of it, a presentiment of what may come.

As an adult, I have experienced that presentiment most vividly while reading two stories: Henry James's *The Turn of the Screw* and Tolstoy's *The Death of Ivan Ilych*. And it was while reading *Ivan Ilych* again, recently, that I began to wonder if the death Tolstoy has Ivan Ilych Golovin experience is anything like the intimation of "death" (or the "beyond") I first caught while imagining children with no faces and women flying across the sky as balls of fire. That is, I wondered if Tolstoy's nineteenth-century conception of death was similar or demonstrably different from my own.

○✧○

Though both were written in the nineteenth century, *The Turn of the Screw* (1898) and *The Death of Ivan Ilych* (1886) belong, at least on the surface, to different genres. Both stories are fixated on the permeable border between life and death, but they were written by men with very different sensibilities. Henry James did not think *War and Peace* was very good — he referred to it as a "loose, baggy monster" — while Tolstoy, if he was familiar with James's sensibility would, likely, have been annoyed by James's hypertrophy of the aesthetic sense. (Tolstoy felt a kind of exasperation for those who went on about the descriptive genius displayed in *Anna Karenin*. And in the end, he began to mistrust his own creative genius, finding it showy and useless in his struggle to strengthen the moral sense of his readers.) And yet, these two stories have some fundamental things in common, the first and most obvious being that they are both ghost stories, though *Ivan Ilych* is rarely thought of as such.

At the beginning of both *The Turn of the Screw* and *The Death of Ivan Ilych*, the character whose story we will follow is dead. There is an element of irony in both cases. The unnamed Governess of *The Turn of the Screw* is obsessed with the reality of the ghosts who may (or may not) be haunting her young wards, while her story — from beyond the grave — is the one that haunts the story's listeners and the book's readers.

In Tolstoy's case, Ivan Ilych Golovin is dead when the story opens. His body is lying in before its burial. After the first chapter, *The Death of Ivan Ilych* becomes a retelling of Ivan Ilych's *life*, but the life recounted by Tolstoy is a death-in-life. Ivan Ilych does not come to real awareness — and thus life — until the moment of his death, which ends the story. Almost literally, Ivan Ilych haunts his own life. He is his own ghost.

A second thing that ties the stories together is their depiction of "inner grotesqueries." Both describe pointedly unpleasant versions of human consciousness. In both, the authors exaggerate negative human responses or describe only those states of mind that are relevant to the mood of the story. In *The Death of Ivan Ilych*, no one — save a servant named Gerasim — is humane, no one curious about anything but his or her own life and fortune. Ilych's wife, Praskovya, is thoughtless and more or less selfish, as is his daughter. *The Death of Ivan Ilych* presents us with a version of life from which almost every speck of altruism has been erased, in the interest of Tolstoy's point: the aloneness of human existence. Tolstoy has created a world in which no one cares about Ivan Ilych, a fact Ivan Ilych belatedly discovers when, while dying, he realizes he is an embarrassment to all those he thought loved him. In a way, it is a story of the enforced loneliness of human existence: no one knows us, nor do we know anyone else; no one understands our pain; we die alone. The Governess of *The Turn of the Screw* is also radically alone. Hers is the *only* perspective we have on the story, hers the only reality. She is trapped in a terrifying solipsism, one in which neither she nor we can tell fact from fancy. No one seems to quite believe her: not the children she is minding, nor Mrs. Grose, her one confidante, nor even the reader, who has plenty of proof that the most terrifying creature in the story is not a ghost but rather the Governess herself. James's Governess and Tolstoy's Ivan Ilych are both prisoners of their own consciousness.

Finally — or "finally" for me, anyway, as I don't mean to exhaustively compare the two stories — both *The Turn of the Screw* and *The Death of Ivan Ilych* are stories which build up to and finish with oddly inflected deaths. In James, the death of a child is ambiguously — not to say obscurely — described:

> . . . "What does he matter now, my own? — what will he ever matter? I have you," I launched at the beast, "but he has lost you for ever!" Then, for the demonstration of my work, "There, *there*!" I said to Miles.
>
> But he had already jerked straight round, stared, glared again, and seen but the quiet day. With the stroke of the loss I was so

proud of he uttered the cry of a creature hurled over an abyss, and the grasp with which I recovered him might have been that of catching him in his fall. I caught him, yes, I held him — it may be imagined with what a passion; but at the end of a minute I began to feel what it truly was that I held. We were alone with the quiet day, and his little heart, dispossessed, had stopped.

In Tolstoy, it is the death of Ivan Ilych himself, which is a "not quite" death, since the end of the story takes us back to its beginning, that is, to Ivan Ilych's funeral.

In place of death there was light.

"So that's what it is!" he suddenly exclaimed aloud. "What joy!"

To him all this happened in a single instant, and the meaning of that instant did not change. For those present his agony continued for another two hours. Something rattled in his throat, his emaciated body twitched, then the gasping and rattle became less and less frequent.

"It's all over!" said someone near him.

He heard these words and repeated them in his soul.

"Death is all over," he said to himself. "It's no more!"

He drew in a breath, stopped in the midst of a sigh, stretched out, and died.

My point in comparing these stories is to suggest that *The Death of Ivan Ilych* achieves some of its effects in the way any ghost story — and *The Turn of the Screw* is one of the best — or frightening tale does: with pace, grotesqueries, intimations of the otherworldly, and a journey to the border between life and death, the place where the dead are living and the living dead. This place is, of course, uncanny and it is akin to the crossroads where the *Soucouyant* must collect and count her grains of rice.[5]

ᏮᎧ

Tolstoy was a master of the significant detail, the detail that sticks because it rings true or because it is odd.

---

5   There is another link between *The Turn of the Screw* and *The Death of Ivan Ilych*, but this one is serendipitous. When the narrator of *The Turn of the Screw* first sees the ghost of her predecessor, it is while looking across at the other side of a small pond facetiously referred to as "The Sea of Azov." The Sea of Azov is, of course, just above the Black Sea. The Ukraine is on one side of it and Russia on the other. So, if you're inclined, you could imagine *The Turn of the Screw*'s Governess looking across at the Russian provinces in which Ivan Ilych lived his death. As I said, it is serendipitous. But it is amusing to imagine that one story haunts the other, as one sensibility is haunted by another.

From Frou-Frou's broken back, in *Anna Karenin*, to Dolokhov sitting on a high window ledge drinking a bottle of rum in one draught, from *War and Peace*, Tolstoy has provided any number of lasting, moving and troubling moments.

Perhaps the most famous image from *The Death of Ivan Ilych* is that of the black bag into which Ivan Ilych Golovin feels he is being pushed:

> For three whole days, during which time did not exist for him, he struggled in that black sack into which he was being thrust by an invisible, resistless force. He struggled as a man condemned to death struggles in the hands of the executioner, though knowing that he cannot save himself. And every moment he felt that despite all his efforts he was drawing nearer and nearer to what terrified him. He felt that his agony was due to being thrust into that black opening and still more to his not being able to get right into it.[6]

---

6   The translation used is by Louise and Aylmer Maude, revised by Bernard Guilbert Guerney for his anthology *A Treasury of Russian Literature*. Guerney did not extensively revise the Maudes' translation, but his is the one recommended by Vladimir Nabokov. The translation by Anthony Briggs (Penguin, 2006) strikes me as less convincing. The 2009 translation by Larissa Volokhonsky and Richard Pevear in the collection *The Death of Ivan Ilych and Other Stories* (Random House) is very good but perhaps faithful to a fault, in that some of its sentences make for so-so English.

This passage leaves us with a visceral idea of dying. It's justly renowned. But I'd like to look at a passage that is much less dramatic, less well known, and slightly puzzling. It is from the story's first chapter, and we are accompanying Ivan Ilych's friend, Peter Ivanovich, as he views his friend's dead body a final time:

Peter Ivanovich, like everyone else on such occasions, entered feeling uncertain what he would have to do. All he knew was that at such times it is always safe to cross oneself. But he was not quite sure whether one should make obeisances while doing so. He therefore adopted a middle course. On entering the room he began crossing himself and made a slight movement resembling a bow. At the same time, as far as the motion of his head and arm allowed, he surveyed the room. Two young men — apparently nephews, one of whom was a high-school pupil — were leaving the room, crossing themselves as they did so. An old woman was standing motionless, and a lady with strangely arched eyebrows was saying something to her in a whisper. A vigorous, resolute clerical person in a frock coat was reading something in a loud voice with an expression that precluded any contradiction. The butler's assistant, Gerasim, stepping lightly in front of Peter Ivanovich, was strewing something on the floor. Noticing this, Peter Ivanovich was immediately aware of the faint odour of a decomposing body.

I read that paragraph over and over until the source of my puzzlement struck me: I wanted to know what it was that Gerasim strewed over the floor. What did the Russians use to cover the smell of dying bodies before the turn of the twentieth century? Moreover, why should Peter Ivanovich become aware of the smell of decomposition after *seeing* Gerasim strew whatever it was he was strewing? Would he not have smelled the corpse first? Or was it, rather, that Gerasim, passing lightly in front of him, stirred the air and so brought the smell of rotting flesh to Peter Ivanovich's notice?

These questions are, relatively, trivial. Tolstoy did not feel he had to be more specific. Towards the end of the first chapter, Peter Ivanovich leaves the house of his dead friend and we read the following:

Peter Ivanovich found the fresh air particularly pleasant after the smells of incense, the dead body, and carbolic acid.

That is, Tolstoy gives a short catalogue of the memorable smells: incense (which Gerasim would not, of course, have been strewing), decomposition, and carbolic acid (used, in the old days, like formaldehyde, to keep the corpse from rotting, though carbolic went out of favour because, though it kept the cells of the dead from decomposing, it turned the skin of the dead an unreal white).[7] Why, I wondered, didn't Tolstoy simply say, "Gerasim was strewing wolf's bane . . ." or "Gerasim was strewing lavender . . ."? Both lavender and wolf's bane (also called monk's hood) were used to cover up the smell of the dead in the nineteenth century.[8]

The mistake I made was, of course, to assume that Gerasim was strewing about something that smelled, something to cover up the smell of putrifaction. If

---

7   I've often wondered why ghosts are white. The idea that a white sheet floating in air could stand in for a ghost is amusing but, also, a little odd. Why should black people, for instance, turn white when they die? Are there no dark-skinned ghosts? Are African ghosts white? And yet, I suppose if you take into account the blood leaving the surface of the skin and the whitening effected by carbolic, you're on the road to seeing the dead as white or whitish. Perhaps the whiteness of a ghost is the end point of our imagination. We see people losing their colour and so understand that the ghost is that entity from which all colour has gone.

8   My mother, born in 1933, remembered seeing her first dead body in 1945, in Trinidad, where she was born. It was the body of her uncle, and she recalled the ice used to keep the corpse from rotting and the smell of carbolic soap. They used lavender in Trinidad to hide bad odours, but they buried her uncle before he had begun to stink and so she had no memory of any specific scent. My father recalled the ice, but he also remembered the use of chlorinated lime, quicklime being used to disinfect any leakage from the dead bodies lying in.

that had been the case, Tolstoy would almost certainly have said so. *The Death of Ivan Ilych* is a work in which smell plays a significant part. No, the important thing in this paragraph was *the sense of smell*, not any specific smell. If you take a look, you'll see that it is a paragraph in which each of the five senses is mentioned or alluded to:

1. Touch: On entering the room he began crossing himself
2. Hearing: ". . . a lady with strangely arched eyebrows was saying something to her in a whisper. A vigorous, resolute clerical person in a frock coat was reading something in a loud voice . . ."
3. Taste: "The butler's assistant, Gerasim, stepping lightly in front of Peter Ivanovich . . ." (or, as Anthony Briggs translates: "Gerasim, the peasant who waited at table . . .")
4. Sight: "Noticing this, Peter Ivanovich was immediately aware . . ." (Louise and Aylmer Maude translated the beginning of the sentence thus: "Seeing this, Pyotr Ivanovich . . .")
5. Smell: "Peter Ivanovich was immediately aware of the faint odour of a decomposing body."

It is a paragraph in which we follow a living being, Peter Ivanovich, whose sentience is insisted on as he approaches the corpse of his childhood friend. Peter Ivanovich touches his forehead as he makes the sign of the cross, hears both soft and loud sounds, remembers seeing Gerasim at the Golovins' dinner table, sees Gerasim strewing something on the floor, and smells the odour of putrescence. (Great word, that: "putrescence" . . .) And yet, in the logic of the story, Peter Ivanovich, though alive and capable of using his senses, is dead in that he is living precisely the kind of death-in-life that Ivan Ilych lived until the moment Ivan Ilych actually died: unwilling to deal with reality (that is, death), careless of any emotions but his own, unable to deal with the suffering of others. In *The Death of Ivan Ilych*, the senses are insufficient signs of life.

Well, what then is *death* — as opposed to death-in-life — in the story?

⚮

Tolstoy gives us a clue to how he felt about the border between life and death when, in his diary, he describes an episode he had while house-hunting in provincial Russia.

In September 1869, Tolstoy spent the night in the town of Arzamas. He was on his way to the province of Penza to look at an estate that interested him. He had just published *War and Peace*, which had brought him fame and money. The journey to Penza was arduous.

His coach broke down. He had to hire horses to continue on his way, and by the time he got to Arzamas, he was too exhausted to go on, and too exhausted to sleep. In a letter to his wife, he wrote:

> It was two o'clock in the morning. I was terribly tired, I wanted to go to sleep and I felt perfectly well. But suddenly I was overcome by despair, fear and terror, the like of which I have never experienced before. I'll tell you all the details of this feeling later: but I've never had such an agonizing feeling before and may God preserve anyone else from experiencing it.

But the fullest account of the incident we have is Tolstoy's unfinished short story called "Diary of a Madman."

"Diary of a Madman" isn't a successful story, but it is a revealing fragment. To begin with, the fear of death is what terrifies the narrator and, significantly, it strikes him while he is away from home, in Arzamas. The narrator is "tormented" by the room in which he must sleep. Here's the passage in Volokhonsky and Pevear's translation:

> A clean, whitewashed, square room. How tormenting it was to me, I remember, that

this little room was precisely square. There was one window, with a curtain — red. A table of Karelian birch and a sofa with curved armrests . . .

The following morning, after an unpleasant, fearful night, things are better once the narrator gets on the road:

In the open air and in movement it got better. But I felt that something new had settled on my soul and poisoned my whole former life.

Once home, the narrator no longer experiences the fear he felt in Arzamas. He begins to pray and attend church, but life goes on as before. And then, some time later, on a trip to Moscow, he stays at an inn. Once again, he is tormented by a room, and this time the fear is worse than it was in Arzamas:

. . . We arrived, I went into the small room. The heavy smell of the corridor was in my nostrils. The porter brought my suitcase. The floor maid lit a candle. The candle flared up, then the flame sank, as always happens. Someone coughed in the next room — probably an old man. The maid left; the porter stood asking if he should undo the straps on my suitcase. The flame revived and threw its light on the blue wallpaper with yellow stripes, a partition, a scratched table, a small sofa, a mirror, a window, and the narrow dimensions of the whole room. And suddenly the whole Arzamas terror stirred in me. "My God, how am I going to spend the night here," I thought.

Perhaps because I've had similar moments of terror and "lostness," I find it fascinating that the narrator's (Tolstoy's) fear of death should be brought on by the condition and dimensions of a room . . .

While I was on an author tour in Minnesota, I woke up in a hotel in Minneapolis and for a good five minutes did not know where I was. The room was indistinguishable from any number of hotel rooms I'd been in, and looking out the window gave me no clue. There was no one for me to call, and it wasn't until I turned on the radio that I came to myself. While I was "lost," it was as if I were adrift in some deserted corner of my own consciousness. The feeling of pure, animal panic reverberated in my psyche for days.

It's difficult to convey the feeling of "lost-ness." It's like a futility and it's like the feeling you have when you're feverish and you think the same thought over and over again. There is a mental agony to the reappearance of the same trees, the same ground, your tracks adding up but leading nowhere. Part of the difficulty, in trying to convey the feeling, is how to suggest both the specific *somewhere* that has become a concrete *nowhere*. It is *somewhere*, because you know it well. You traverse it over and over. Your footprints are there. You know the place. You start to recognize the trees and the ground. And yet, it is not a place. It is a *not-home*. It is, suddenly, a part of the world cut off from the world: nowhere and somewhere at once. A place with which you are unwillingly, inescapably intimate. The place is itself a kind of violation of your consciousness, of your self.[9]

Here's how Tolstoy describes being lost:

---

9   I can find no particular name for this feeling. "Atopy," the Greek word, is almost right, if you take it literally. *Topos* is the Greek for "place." So, *Atopy* — as an English word — should mean, literally, nowhere-ness. But the word *atopy* has come to refer to originality, a thing or person so unusual as to be thought of as coming from no known place. (Curiously, *atopy* also refers to a predisposition to skin rash brought on by exposure to dust mites, dander, insect venom, and other common irritants.) If we try to make a word using Latin, we start with *nusquam* ("no place"). But any English word from *nusquam* (like, say, "nusquamness," which sounds like a town in British Columbia, or "nusquamity," which is awkward) is difficult to imagine as part of common speech. .

. . . And suddenly I felt I was lost. Home, the hunters were far away, nothing could be heard. I was tired and all in a sweat. Once you stop, you freeze. If you keep walking, you lose strength. I called out, all was quiet. No one responded. I walked back again. My legs were tired. I felt frightened, stopped, and the whole terror of Arzamas and Moscow came over me, only a hundred times greater. My heart pounded, my arms and legs trembled. To die here? I don't want to. Why die? What is death? I wanted to question, to reproach God as before, but here I suddenly felt that I didn't dare, that I shouldn't, that I couldn't have accounts with God, that he had said what was needed, that I alone was to blame.

I take it that this is the *feeling* at the heart of *The Death of Ivan Ilych*, the feeling that lies at the heart of the "death" Tolstoy speaks of: the sensation of being nowhere, of being lost. But in *The Death of Ivan Ilych*, Tolstoy doesn't refer to lostness directly. Ivan Ilych does not die in a foreign city or in a forest. He dies at home, but it is a "home" which has become foreign, an "un-home" that is as terrifying as nowhere, a "home" stripped of the possibility of belonging.

Just as life and death have exchanged places in *The Death of Ivan Ilych* (living being a form of death, death being a form of life), so too have belonging and lostness. There where he should feel he has a place — that is, in his own home — Ivan Ilych Golovin comes to feel lost: alienated from the affections of his wife, daughter, and son, a problem for his servants, a speck of disorder in this place (his home) where he had thought himself the *origin* of order, the father, the one on whom "home" depends:[10]

> . . . Whether it was morning or evening, Friday or Sunday, was all the same, all one and the same: a gnawing tormenting pain, never subsiding for a moment; the awareness of life ever hopelessly going but never quite gone; always the same dreadful, hateful death approaching — the sole reality now — and always the same lie. What were days, weeks and hours here?
>
> "Would you care for tea, sir?"
>
> "He needs order, so his masters should have tea in the mornings," [Ivan Ilych] thought, and said only:

10   There is an added irony here: in the story, Tolstoy has Ivan Ilych mortally wound himself precisely while he is trying to create a home for his family.

"No."

"Would you like to lie on the sofa?"

"He needs to tidy up the room, and I'm in the way, I am uncleanness, disorder," he thought, and said only

"No, let me be."

So, there it is: nowhere home. No longer belonging where he once belonged, Ivan Ilych Golovin is in transit.

❧

I began this essay, among other reasons, because I wondered if the "death" Tolstoy imagined in *The Death of Ivan Ilych* was like the "death" nestled in my own imagination. I assumed, to be honest, that "death" for a northerner (that is, Tolstoy), with its snows and lakes and wolves, would be different from the "death" in the mind of a South American (that is, myself, though Trinidad isn't quite South America): mountains, floods, poisonous snakes. I'm still convinced there is a cultural difference in how we figure "death," but the more I read the story, following its sense through the translations of Louise and Aylmer Maude, Bernard Guerney's revision of the Maudes, Anthony Briggs, and Volokhonsky and Pevear, the more I came to feel that Tolstoy and I do have something in common: the idea of "death" as the foreignness of "home." That is, I've come to see that one of the reasons *The Death of Ivan Ilych* has meant so much to me, one of the reasons it has held my attention through the decades since I first read it, one of the reasons I read it over and over, is that it articulates a nightmare of my immigrant's consciousness. Its truth is the truth not of "death" (whatever that might be) but of something else:

The end of all travel is to be nowhere.

SAMUEL BECKETT,
OR ON RECONCILIATION

After my breakup with K, I was bitter and disappointed,
and I wrote poetry:

On certain days, torn apart and wounded,
the silence between us caustic enough to scald
metal, I would find reason to walk by your home.

On those days, the flowers in your back garden,
the sight of Echinacea, made me cough
as if I had swallowed the plants whole
and could feel, fingers on throat,
their unwilling passage down.
On these days, I'd brace myself against
your peremptory affection,
Your dark eyebrows tamed by your index finger.

How had I managed to fall in love with such a cold cup of lye?
Was it the cup or the lye that seduced me?

And let me just say, now those days are gone,
they were not the worst between us.

I think I understand this will to poetry. For one thing, K is a poet, so poetry was my way of speaking to her, though she was no longer there. For another, poetry is — at times — a means of exhausting hurtful emotions, or turning them to ash. The process isn't efficient, nor immediately effective, however. So, looking for further distraction, I went to Pages and bought, though I couldn't really afford them, the four volumes of Samuel Beckett's *Collected Works*, edited by Paul Auster.

Beckett: not the place one would go for solace, you'd think.

But Samuel Beckett is one of the reasons I have spent so much of my life writing. His work has always brought me solace, and when I began to read through the novels, two things brought pleasure as well as consolation. First, there were the words: *infundibular, gehenna, absterge, podex, narthex*. Reading the novels (*Murphy, Watt, Molloy, Malone Dies, The Unnamable, How It Is*), I was reacquainted with words that had stayed with me (*gehenna, absterge, podex*) and words that had not (*narthex* . . . I still can't recall its meaning without a dictionary, and I looked it up just the other day). Second, Beckett's work is filled with descriptions of place, with hills, fields, woods, and seashores. So much so that the novels themselves feel like a country to which I have citizenship.

And, feeling at home, I read two thousand pages in a fortnight.

Reading Beckett, I was not distracted from anger or grief. Rather, I was exposed to a suffering (Beckett's) that had consequences for my own, a suffering that brought about a confrontation with my own emotions, and it's in that confrontation that I found distraction and solace and the beginning of something else . . . a reconciliation.

❦

In a collection of essays called *The Broken Estate*, the literary critic James Wood writes often about "the real." The "real" is, he implies, *the* touchstone for all writers. Even the Surrealists, in Wood's account, start from the "real" world, and their literary effectiveness is dependent on their readers' familiarity with it. That is, readers, having the real world before them, can appreciate unusual versions of it. For Wood, Surrealism is a kind of funhouse mirror. This idea is, I think, the least convincing aspect of *The Broken Estate.* To begin with,

Wood's versions of "real" and "realism" aren't stable. He uses the words to mean very different things. But he also ignores that, in their quest to *represent* the world, writers (all artists, really) respond to other *representations* of the world at least as deeply as they respond to the "real" world itself. These other representations are as important — at times *more* important — for the creation (and appreciation) of a work of art as the "real" world is.

> It was on a road remarkably bare, I mean without hedges or ditches or any kind of edge, in the country, for cows were chewing in enormous fields, lying and standing, in the evening silence.
>
> — *Molloy* (*Collected Works*, Vol. 2)

For writers, like myself, who have been influenced by Samuel Beckett, the situation is something like this: I know that Beckett's version of landscape leaves out more than it includes — necessarily, since the simplest view contains a million details. At the beginning of *Molloy*, when the narrator describes a near encounter on a "bare" road, he uses a handful of nouns to represent the vast countryside he is describing: cows, fields, hills, sea, dew, sky. It's an affecting and beautiful description of Ireland, and I think it has influenced both how I look at landscape and what I choose to include when I describe one.

Though I grew up in Canada (Ottawa, mostly, but also Petrolia, Ontario), and though my descriptions of landscape include elements that Beckett's do not, there has been, from the moment I first read *Molloy*, something irreducibly Beckettian about my world and about my representations of the world. Of course, "Beckettian" is not a simple designation. I'm reminded of an anecdote told by Israel Horovitz. Horovitz was in Paris to give a reading of his poetry. He had not invited Beckett, because Beckett did not go to public readings. But when Beckett found out about the reading, he asked Horovitz to read him, privately, a poem. The poem Horovitz read included the line "Our love lives within the space of a quietly closing door." Having read the line, Horovitz said

— Oh, shit!

Beckett asked him what was wrong.

— I stole that line from you, said Horovitz.

— I never heard it before in my life, said Beckett.

Horovitz quoted from Beckett's poem "Dieppe," which ends with the line "the space of a door that opens and shuts."

— Oh, yes, that's true, said Beckett

but then *he* suddenly said

— Oh, shit!

— What's the matter? asked Horovitz.

— I stole it from Dante me-self, Beckett answered.

Yes, exactly. We take from the artists we admire.

And so, to a certain extent, it is with Beckett's landscapes as well. His way of looking and representing comes from Dante, who comes from Virgil, who comes from Homer, who comes from some anonymous poet who travelled and sang for his (or her) living, and so on. However far back one goes, there is never the world-in-itself, never the simply real. There is always an artistry. Writers come from somewhere and that somewhere includes innumerable depictions of somewhere else.

Still, representing the world, as opposed to the emotions, is *almost* a technical matter. The task is to create a credible and vivid impression of a world, without boring the reader. What one learns from Beckett or Dante or whomever is a way of discriminating in kind as well as number of details. Had I been more deeply influenced by Dostoyevsky, say, my version of landscape would have been more melodramatic — rain, cloud, mist obscuring the day when one of my characters meets his or her obscure fate. More influenced by Hardy, my landscape would become a character: sullen, dark, almost overbearing; more influenced by Homer, landscapes are repetitive, simple, talismanic.

For a writer, the world is an aesthetic proposition as much as it is a thing to touch.

Travelling to Saint John, shortly after I had broken with K, I wrote

> By morning light,
> the trunk of a young beech
> rises from the black ground
> like whitish smoke.

> I am on a train,
> alone, between
> Matapédia and Campbellton.

Now, if it is true that what I see of my world is influenced by Beckett's way of seeing, is it also true that my *feelings* are Beckettian? It's one thing to organize the visual world based on another's example, but it's a little unnerving to contemplate Beckett's influence on my emotional self. Is my unhappiness not my own, then? Am I miserable, when I am miserable, according to another's misery?

No, I don't think so. Though I feel close to certain aspects of Beckett's world view, Beckett and I are among the millions and millions whose minds naturally incline to the dark. Besides, as humans, we're inheritors of an unshakable privacy. My emotions and my world are my own, until I've represented them. It's only *then* that I can see them as "Beckettian," only then that I can say, "Look, this turn of phrase — 'the trunk of a young beech' — sounds like it comes from *Molloy* or *Krapp's Last Tape*," though, of course, Beckett never saw the land on the way to Campbellton: the grey-blue water, the small houses on one bank looking over at the houses on the other shore, the bleached light of a winter morning in New Brunswick.

This mix-up of private and represented (my emotions and my writing of them) is something that happens often as I read Beckett. His is a work I'm able to lose myself in. And, I suppose, this lostness in Beckett casts an interesting light on Israel Horovitz's embarrassment at the thought he had stolen from Beckett. An emotion of his own, something deeply personal, had been unwittingly expressed with an image taken from Beckett. It must have felt as if his deepest self were not quite his.

Beckett responded, kindly and with great wit, by pointing to Dante.

But was Horovitz comforted, I wonder, by the thought that the image ("an open door") had come "first" from Dante?

◌◌◌

I read through Beckett's *Collected Works* with women and "love" in mind.

It's difficult to tell from Beckett's fiction what his attitude to women was. It's probably impossible. The mixture, in fiction, of psyche and intellect is different from author to author. We can't say when Beckett was being serious, or joking, or half-joking. Fiction is the kind of play that requires all strata of consciousness, but it takes from the strata in different proportions from one work to the next.

Still, there *are* "women" in Beckett's fiction and, in general, they are not like the "men." Where Beckett's men are wary, mistrustful, impotent, unsure of the line between love and sex, his women are optimistic, sexual, long-suffering, and hopeful. At times, the struggle between the sexes is cast as a struggle between metaphysical ideals (which the men pursue) and the demands of the world (which the women accept).

To stay with the "men": there is in Beckett's work a hyper-consciousness of the body in decline. His male narrators live to either note or chart the body's decay: teeth go missing, feet hurt, walking becomes difficult without crutches, locomotion impossible without a bicycle, sexual arousal an inconvenience. It's little surprise, then, that the descriptions of sexual intimacy in his work are not joyous. But there are also, in all the "male"-narrated works, meditations on love and intimacy. In fact, horror of the body, or the body's failings, often presage or accompany moments of metaphysical

149

longing. This passage from the story "First Love" is exemplary:

> But man is still today, at the age of twenty-
> five, at the mercy of an erection, physically
> too, from time to time, it's the common
> lot, even I was not immune, if that may be
> called an erection. It did not escape her,
> naturally, women smell a rigid phallus ten
> miles away and wonder, How on earth did
> he spot me from there? One is no longer
> oneself, on such occasions, and it is pain-
> ful to be no longer oneself, even more pain-
> ful, if possible, than when one is. For when
> one is one knows what to do to be less so,
> whereas when one is not one is any old
> one irredeemably. What goes by the name
> of love is banishment, with now and then
> a postcard from the homeland, such is my
> considered opinion, this evening.
>
> "First Love" (*Collected Works*, Vol. 4)

What goes by the name of love is banishment . . . ?
Naturally, given my anger and grief and longing
for K, I found this passage striking for its revelation
of love as banishment. But it's even more striking in
the context of Beckett's work. Despite this passage's

insinuation that homelessness (or alienation from the self) is an *unwanted* consequence of loving, Beckett's work is filled with narrators who long for nothing less than this very banishment, this escape from the self. Murphy, protagonist of the novel *Murphy*, seeks to escape the prison that is his body for a kind of pure empyrean of soul and nothingness. A number of the other narrators (Molloy in particular) express disgust with the "self" they are stuck with. So, in the context of Beckett's work, this passage could be read as a contradiction, perhaps even as the expression of a secret longing for the "un-self-ing" that comes with lust.

But wait. Let's go back to that passage from "First Love," to break it down a little. The narrator says:

1. Men can not avoid desire.
2. Women are attuned to desire.
3. When desiring, a man is no longer "himself."
4. Being other than oneself is painful because
    a. being oneself is something one is used to and, thus, something one can *do* something about. It is a curable condition.
    b. being someone else, someone *other* than oneself means being no one in particular or "any old one" and how is one to live then?

Up to this point, everything is clear, and then comes

5. *Love* is a form of banishment.

How and where did we pass from desire to "love"? That's the jump my mind made as I read that passage, but of course we do not pass from *desire* to *love*. Beckett wrote "*What goes by the name* of love." The banishment he is referring to is brought on by his erection. Love, *real* love, the thing that has no name, here, in this passage, is not banishment. "Real love" is, perhaps, *homecoming*, that which eludes the narrator of "First Love," precisely the thing Murphy seeks when he ties himself, by means of seven scarves, to his rocking chair and goes in search of the unattainable *place*.

Rereading Beckett, I encountered what I thought of as my "literary self" over and over again, but the idea of love as banishment, or *desire* as banishment, reminded me of something I'd written immediately after my break-up with K:

> A calm comes over me after we've made love
> You've turned away and your back gracefully
> declines. How fascinating this is: light
> from a candle, the smell of us exhaled
> by a bedsheet. But all of this must end.
> In a moment, you'll rise to wipe my semen
> from your belly. The cats will tilt against
> your shins, in their cloudy campaign for food.
> And so a door will close. I'd hold us here
> a moment more, but desire dies

in the time it takes you to turn and ask
if I'm hungry. I say something clever
and meaningless and close a door myself,
as you yawn and go to the kitchen.

It's disconcerting to write such things, to *feel* them
about a relationship that has ended. For months, my
memory was like a white, tile floor on which clear
glass has broken. But the banishment described in
this poem is of a different order from that described
in "First Love." The state of pleasure after lovemaking
is a kind of alienation from the self, yes, but most of
us would prolong this alienation if we could. To me,
the banishment is less extraordinary than the place to
which I have been permitted access, the place where
I am not my "self," the place where I can live without
regard for my endless names or the many selves they
designate.

Very lovely, but what am I saying, exactly? That
the moments following lovemaking are what I know
of love? That although desire un-selfs us, once desire
is spent we may come to another, deeper place? Isn't
this a convenient conflation of love and desire, with
the emphasis on what *follows* orgasm as opposed to
the great derangement that precedes it? And what
is it about the postcoital moment that suggests love,
anyway?

As a man who rarely feels at home in the world, the intimacy, the two-in-oneness that follows lovemaking is one of the only states during which I am will-lessly taken from myself. It isn't inevitable, you understand. I've certainly had sex and felt nothing but embarrassment afterwards, ashamed that I had allowed myself to be vulnerable. This "world of two as one" (an occlusion of myself) has come into being with only three women in my life. The three I have loved — meaning, I suppose, the three with whom I was not careful to hold to my "self."

In love, I couldn't care less who I am or who I am not.

Yes, the banishment in my poem is almost entirely different from the banishment in "First Love." Nevertheless, when I read Beckett again, I felt he had articulated something within me. Behind my "banishment," there is Beckett's.

A predecessor's use of an image (or notion) doesn't cancel out one's own use of the same image (or notion). Each *use* of a figure or image is like a veil before the thing itself: a small brass key on a table of white wood, say. Every writer puts a veil in front the table and key, a veil that is like a fine Dacca gauze ("Those transparent Dacca gauzes / known as woven air, running / water, evening dew . . . ," as Agha Shahid Ali wrote). One is always aware of the key and the table, but one sometimes becomes aware of all the veils before them, too.

And isn't it odd that artists so often point to a specific veil (Dante's, for instance) and say "this veil has meant so much to me"?

⁂

There are any number of ways to express the unhappiness that follows the end of a relationship. The images that come to me bring with them the idea of place (garden, field, bedroom) and discomfort therein. The feeling for place and place lost is often found in Beckett's work. So, when I speak of Beckett's "influence" on my writing, I suppose I'm referring to my sometimes unconscious appropriation of his images (fields, rooms, etc.) and language to express my own feelings.

"Influence" is a mercurial word, though. Not only does the assertion of influence beg the question "where does this image or idea come from in the first place?" but it also implies that the one who has been influenced, the ephebe, has come to his or her world of symbols through the agency of *this* master's work and this master's work alone. But the idea that the ephebe needs a *specific* master in order to produce his or her work is a little unconvincing. I mean, it's difficult to think of any artwork that has had anything but *multiple* progenitors. Then, too, there are the natures of the master and the ephebe. If they are both exiles (as Beckett and Dante both were), isn't it likely that they will turn to and

155

respond to similar images? Dante loved Homer's *Odyssey*, while Beckett admired Joyce's *Ulysses*. A school of exiles — Homer, Dante, Joyce, Beckett. Is it so surprising they should have images and ideas (banishment, exile, loss) in common? Is it inconceivable that they might come to the same images and ideas independently? It would be stranger, wouldn't it, for those who share Dante's emotional type or some of his circumstances, *not* to sound like Dante once in a while.

And yet, Beckett *insists* on Dante. He is one of those writers who inevitably points away from himself. In fact, we can be confident that Beckett was influenced by Dante not only because we hear echoes of Dante in Beckett's writing but because Beckett has so vigorously asserted Dante's presence. He has *leaned* on Dante's influence. He wrote an essay entitled "Dante . . . Bruno. Vico . . . Joyce" linking his masters Dante and James Joyce; his short story "Dante and the Lobster" is filled with references to the *Divine Comedy*; he referred to the novels *Molloy*, *Malone Dies*, and *The Unnamable* as being tripartite, in the way of Dante's *Comedy*. In fact, one of the most striking aspects of Beckett's thinking may well be this obsession with his own lack of innovation.[11]

---

11   Beckett's characters are as obsessive as he is on this score. They regularly disavow responsibility for the words they speak. They refuse to admit they have any creativity. They compare themselves to mechanicals whose only work is the turning of a tap: on or off (see *Cascando*, for instance).

So insistent is Beckett in pointing to Dante, I decided to re-read *La Vita Nuova*, Dante's brilliant, prosimetric[12] meditation on love and poetry, to discover just how much Beckett I could glean from it. Here is a passage from the *Canzone* that begins with the words "*Donna pietosa*." In it, Dante describes the "doubtful" landscape of premonition and bereavement:

> Lying there, thinking of the fragility of my life,
> seeing how slight its substance is,
> Love, whose home is in my heart, began to weep:
> at which my soul was so distraught
> that sighing I said in my thoughts:
> "It is true that my lady too will die."
> Then I was so filled with distress,
> I closed my eyes, so heavy were they with that abyss.
> And so scattered
> were my spirits, they all went wandering:
> and then imagination,
> roaming wildly and far from truth,
> showed me women's faces hurrying by
> that cried to me: "You will die, you will die."

---

12 A prosimetrum is a literary work made up of passages of poetry and prose. For example: Basho's *Narrow Road to the Deep North*, Boethius's *Consolation of Philosophy*, Nabokov's *Pale Fire*, and, of course, this essay, which was written with *La Vita Nuova* very much in mind.

Then I saw many doubtful things,
in the empty dream I had entered:
I seemed to be in a place I did not know,
and saw women going by in the street,
dishevelled, weeping, crying out,
their cries spread like fires of grief.
Then it seemed to me little by little
the sun darkened and the stars appeared,
and they wept together as one:
birds fell as they flew through the air,
and the earth trembled:
And a pale man appeared and, hoarse,
said to me: "What? Have you not heard the news?
Your lady is dead, who was so lovely."[13]

After rereading *La Vita Nuova*, I began a comparison of Beckett's banishment from the self and Dante's banishment from Love. And there are certainly echoes (as well as perversions, parodies, and deformations) of Dante in Beckett. They both have versions of courtly love, versions of love as transcendent and redemptive (though, in Beckett's case, the redemption is endlessly deferred), versions of banishment and bereavement, and so on. The resonances — some of which you can hear clearly if you

---

13   This translation of *La Vita Nuova* was modified from that of A. S. Kline (copyright 2001). Modifications by André Alexis.

read "First Love" and *La Vita Nuova* together — appealed to me. But the more I went about comparing the two, the more I felt I had fallen into a trap. Beckett's insistence on Dante is misleading. Let me count the ways:

1. Though James Joyce had a great influence on Beckett's work (again, Beckett *dixit*), the insistence on Dante serves to obscure Joyce's influence. In pointing out Dante's influence on Joyce, Beckett goes one step further, dissolving Joyce in Dante.
2. By insisting on Dante's influence, Beckett enshadows influences that are less "elevated," though perhaps as significant (Buster Keaton, Stephen Leacock, etc.)
3. By insisting on Dante, Beckett provides a kind of clarity — an explanation for why he writes as he does — that makes his work *less* complicated than it actually is.
4. By insisting on Dante, Beckett gets to have it both ways: he disappears behind Dante while remaining ever-present as "he who points to Dante."

That third point was the most intriguing and most perplexing, as far as I was concerned. Why would Beckett want to make his work seem less complicated than it is?

By constantly pointing to Dante, to Dante's influence, Beckett is insisting on his own *critical* — as opposed to creative — intelligence, on his awareness (even if it is sometimes unconscious) of his (that is, Beckett's) place in a literary spectrum. We know, however, that Beckett trusted his unconscious, that he gave it free rein. He compared his writing process to that of the Surrealists, saying he began with the pure stuff of his subconscious and then *worked* it into the shape he wished.

Is it possible that he *inevitably* worked his creations towards Dante?

If so, how did he know he was working towards Dante and no one else? Dante himself was aware of his own debts to Virgil, Guido Cavalcanti, and Statius (to keep only to poets whom Dante admitted to admiring). In being influenced by Dante, how influenced was Beckett by Cavalcanti or Virgil or Publius Statius?

It's easy, isn't it, to imagine a dialogue between Dante and Beckett in which Dante says

— *Cazzo, anch'io l'ho copiato, da Stazio!*[14]

And that's it, isn't it? The *main* problem with the idea of "influence" is that it leads, inevitably, to questions of priority that can't be answered. And though the effort to designate who has influenced whom is amusing and sometimes enlightening, especially when made by a critic like Borges,[15] the effort probably has less to

---

14 "Shit! I stole it from Statius me-self."

15 Borges was the first to speak of "reverse influence," the idea that as Kafka's work influences our reading of Dickens, it allows us to identify the

do with understanding what it is men and women do when they use words symbolically than it has to do with power and status.[16] That is to say, the creation of an echelon of influence, with Dante at the top, or Homer, or Shakespeare, is more significant as politics than aesthetics. It has nothing to do with the beautiful.

⬭

If reading *La Vita Nuova* did not (*could* not) tell me why Beckett needed Dante as such a constant point of reference, it did start me thinking about reconciliation, its nature and variations.

La Vita Nuova is a work of mourning, autobiography and literary criticism. In it, Dante tells of his love for Beatrice. He chooses a number of his poems about her, commenting on them and on the poetic tradition to which they belong. The most striking poem in it, for me, is the *Canzone* from which I've quoted, the one that begins "*Donna pietosa*." It is a poem that prefigures the death of Beatrice and leads to the end of the book, in

---

Kafkaesque in Dickens. So, we can as meaningfully speak of Kafka's influence on Dickens as of Dickens's influence on Kafka.

16 An aside: how many ways are there for a writer to be original? While rereading Beckett and *La Vita Nuova*, I could come up with only two fairly bland versions of originality:

    1. use the material you have in a new way formally (from sonnet to Shakespearean sonnet, from story to detective story, etc.)

which the poet is actually bereft of Beatrice. *La Vita Nuova* is, above all, a meditation on love (courtly love) as the highest virtue, goal, or attainment. The fact of Beatrice's death is overwhelming, but through poetry it has been transformed. The love Dante has for Beatrice is enshrined in the poetry along with the grief at her death. Poetry allows Dante to go on, by bringing the two emotions together, by reconciling life and death.

(A definition: *reconciliation* comes from the Latin verb *conciliare* — "to bring together," "to unite." It means to "re-bring together" or to unite once again. Reconciliation can also refer to the process of making consistent or compatible, like seamlessly gluing two halves of a broken plate together again.)

---

2. think of the material you use in a new way (concrete poetry, sound poetry, etc.)

The problem, I think, is that I confused "originality" and "innovation." The man or woman who first used language poetically was being original; all others have innovated. *Origin* comes from the Latin word *origo*, which means "beginning." The phrase *fons et origo* means (or is translated as) "source and beginning." The word *innovation* comes from the Latin word *novus*, which means "new." Ezra Pound's exhortation to the writer to "make it new" is an encouragement to do the one thing we can do: use the material we have inherited in a slightly different way. Pound is exhorting writers to do precisely what the greats who preceded us have done: renew the possibilities of the art, leave an unforgettable stamp. We are to do, over and again, what has been done a thousand times before. And fair enough: a new version of old or an old version of new.

But to get back to that "man or woman who first used language poetically" . . .

There's no originality (in the sense of a beginning) there either, I think. The "man or woman who first used language poetically" is pure fiction.

Beckett's work cannot and does not effect a reconciliation. In that sense, he is Dante's mirror opposite. Beckett's work is filled with longing for the reconciliation at the heart of Dante's art. Beckett's characters constantly tell their stories, with the hope that . . . in the belief that if they can only tell their stories "right," they will be relieved of the burden of telling. They are optimists, in that they never stop believing that there *will* be a moment of transcendence, that a life freed of the need to speak will come, that when there is no more need for Art, they and life will be, finally at peace, finally reconciled. The art by which Dante found reconciliation is impossible for Beckett, but Beckett's work makes a virtue of its yearning for the "impossible," and so keeps

---

I mean, I can't at all believe in the moment when one suddenly looked up and said something "poetic" to another or to herself. For one thing, this suggests a rigid line between poetic and non-poetic speech. (Walter Benjamin's dictum that great poetry springs from great prose — speech, for instance — seems undeniably true, to me at any rate.) For another, it suggests that Poetry (understood as language used for aesthetic effect) came into being in one extraordinarily auspicious moment. Is that credible? No, I think Language itself is the *fons et origo* of Poetry. Poetry and prose (not quite arbitrarily separated) spring from the nature of language. All of us who use language are (at times) helplessly poetic. Poetry is an endless recurrence of the same, of the thing within language or the aspect of language that will out. Writers, and speakers too, exploit this aspect of language (or is it, rather, this *flaw* in language?). Poets draw our attention to it most insistently. On this model, the poetic is rather like the yellow and red motes of fire that dance above a fireplace. One wouldn't say the fire "intends" them, though they are inevitable and captivating. The artist, the one who builds the fire, has intention. His or her intent may be the warmth or the motes, or both the warmth *and* the motes, but none is at the origin of fire.

the "impossible" (reconciliation) as firmly in mind as Dante's work does.

But if, in his *art*, Beckett could not arrive at transcendence or reconciliation, in his attitude to the past he may have. By endlessly pointing to Dante as his master, Beckett is doing two things. First, he is suggesting that his ideal Art is one exemplified by Dante's work. And second, by constantly placing himself in relation to the past, by constantly bringing himself into line with Dante, by stressing the dependence of his work on Dante's, he is like a man swimming a great distance from shore who must look back to see where he is or else go too far and drown.

This looking back, finding perspective, placing himself on an echelon, was, perhaps, Beckett's way of making sense of an otherwise futile endeavour (Art). In his work, he embraced the futility. He made the futility his subject. But in talking about his literary "place" — somewhere *after* Dante — he was able to connect with (or place himself in an acceptable relationship to) a human striving (Art/Literature) for which he felt evident love *and* ambivalence.

I asked a couple of questions near the beginning of this essay. I answer them, now, with the idea of reconciliation in mind.

1. Are my images my own?

No, not really. Most will have been used before me by writers who have preceded me. Or if, in fact, an "object-image" of mine is new, the *mode* of its use will not be unusual. That is, for want of the telephone, Dante could not have written Cocteau's *Voix humaine*, but he would have understood Cocteau's work as one poet understands another's. In this sense, all poets are contemporaries. Shakespeare might not immediately appreciate bpNichol's concrete poems, but I bet it wouldn't take him long to understand what it is that makes bp's work necessary.

2. Are my emotions my own?

Certainly, and they are private. Much as I might wish otherwise, no one knows what I am feeling until I express my feelings in a language. But once they're expressed, once they are written, their privacy is compromised.[17]

---

17 I was originally asked to write this essay on Beckett by Michael Redhill for *Brick* magazine. After some debate, the editors of *Brick* declined to publish the essay. I had a note from Michael Redhill expressing his regret at the board's decision, but there were two reasons the piece could not be accepted. First, some of the editors found the essay too "academic" for *Brick*. A good reason, I think, and I wish they'd left it at that. (After all, to "fail" when writing about Beckett is almost to succeed.)

Their second reason, however, was bewildering. *Brick*'s editors felt that the poems (the poems in particular) would hurt the woman with whom I had, two years previously, broken up, the woman they *assumed* was the "K" referred to in the essay. They did not know whom the essay was *actually* about, but they assumed they knew, because the Toronto literary scene is small, inbred, and provincial. Michael wrote me that,

Wondering what I loved most about you, I broke
a bâtard and brushed its crumbs from the tablecloth.

What were you thinking, as you pushed the sugar bowl
away, touched the rim of your cup,
turned to look out the window of La Gamelle?

That fragment of time has an orbit
now, returning at intervals,
eclipsing the present.

I have broken the same bâtard
a thousand times, watched you
push the sugar bowl and look out the window,

---

in his opinion, whomever the essay was *actually* about was immaterial.
People in the community, and "K" herself, would *assume* it referred to her,
and that — coupled with the essay's academic tone — was enough to put
them off. The editorial board did not feel that they could knowingly hurt
someone who was bound to be upset by the personal nature of the revelations contained in the essay.

Now, the essay *was* about the woman in question, but only to an
extent. It was also about *another* woman entirely, one with whom I had
more recently broken up. And it was also about my first love, my break-up
with whom deeply marked my sensibility. So, the poems were written
about *three* women, not one. And the André Alexis in question was not
entirely me, either. For one thing, I find the emotional devastation that
follows the end of a relationship too difficult a place to write from.

If the editors of *Brick* had not known me, if they had had no idea
whom I was referring to, would they have had the same qualms about the
piece? I don't think so. They would still have found the Beckett commentary "academic" and the first poem would still have struck them as bitter,
but I don't believe they'd have moved to protect someone who did not

a thousand times. I have not left you,
not made you unhappy, not destroyed our life
together.

Then comes the revolution:
I have left, I have made again, I have destroyed.
A thousand times and one.

For meaning, meaningless.
Even for meaningless, meaningless,
this persistent moment. But I miss your hands.
And that is more than I knew then.

These words connect me to poets who have written
before me. (It isn't the quality of the work that connects

---

exist for them. Michael Redhill, in a post to me, insisted that I'm wrong to
believe this, that the tone of the piece would have put them off, would have
forced them to protect this unknown woman at the heart of the bitter first poem.

But take a look at the poems (at the "personal material") again. The
first poem, which begins "On certain days," is, indeed, bitter. But its bitterness is what one would expect after a breakup, no? The second poem,
"By morning light," is written in the style of a Japanese poem — consciously
minimalist, moving towards Beckettian. No woman is mentioned. The
third poem, "A calm comes over me," is revealing, but revealing of the
state of bliss that follows lovemaking. It is filled with regret and longing.
These are, surely, *not* offensive things to feel about a woman. But, in any
case, the poem is not about "K" at all. The final poem begins "Wondering
what I loved." It is a poem of *enduring* affection, written with *three* women
in mind, the "moment" in it pure invention. So, bitterness, heartbreak,
longing, love, and reconciliation with the past: a sequence of emotions
that (*pointedly*) underlies the progress of the essay itself, from the bitterness
of the first poem to the grief transformed at the heart of Dante's *La Vita Nuova*.

me. It's the fact of it. They also separate me from my predecessors. The poem is both new and old, as are the emotions that inspired it. In this back and forth, something essential takes place, something that is likely to go on for years, as I try to come to terms with the aesthetic quality of the poem and the emotional pain that lies behind it.

There is a final reconciliation to talk about: the (hopefully skilful) bringing together of elements or ideas to create this essay, elements and ideas inspired by my most recent reading of Beckett's work:

> — A new life comes only once you have seen the old life for what it is. For this, poetry can be invaluable.
> — Seeing the history of literature with himself firmly in place beside Dante was Beckett's way of placing himself in relationship to the past.
> — Understanding that Beatrice is dead, Dante can go on, only after turning her death into a sort of permanence, a permanence that allows consoling "repair" of the breach that Beatrice's death has created in his life and his soul.
> — Seeing oneself "in relation to" a person,

      a lineage, a tragic event (rather than being
      trapped in the emotions called up by them):
      this is the beginning of reconciliation.

I began this essay wanting simply to talk about Beckett, a writer who has meant much to me, as a way to avoid the emotions brought on by heartbreak. But rereading Beckett, taking the consolation his work offers (humour, a mirror, distraction), has had the effect of bringing me to think about the connection between "solace" and "reconciliation," the solace one (*sometimes*) feels when one sees clearly where one is *and* where one has been. That is, the solace that comes when one is able to bring together, for instance, the end of a relationship and the moment when heartbreak begins to heal, or the first time one reads a writer (like Beckett) and the latest reading of him (which is another way of bringing two of one's many selves together), or the moment of Dante's greatest pain (at Beatrice's death) and that moment's transcendence through art (*La Vita Nuova*). Being able to hold two or more things together at once: that's the reconciliation I have in mind, here.

WATER: A MEMOIR

... home is just a place you started out, the only place
you still know how to think from, so that that place is
mated to this by necessity as well as choice ...
— Roo Borson, *Summer Grass*

Thinking from Home

I had a wonderful grade-thirteen English teacher
named Mr. Holloway. He introduced us to the Canadas
of *Fifth Business*, *The Stone Angel*, *The Luck of Ginger
Coffey*, and *The Apprenticeship of Duddy Kravitz*. And
having discovered various versions of the world outside my door, I wanted to explore literary Canada for
myself.

During my first year at Carleton University, I
avoided the books I was supposed to read and, instead,
read all the Canadian work I could. I discovered George

Bowering, Michael Ondaatje, Earle Birney, Margaret Avison, Irving Layton, Leonard Cohen, Dorothy Livesay. Poets, mostly, and the poet who mattered most was Margaret Atwood. For weeks, I listened obsessively to a recording of her reading from her own work. I had her voice in my head. In fact, I had a particular poem in my head: "This Is a Photograph of Me."

This Is a Photograph of Me

It was taken some time ago.
At first it seems to be
a smeared
print: blurred lines and grey flecks
blended with the paper;

then, as you scan
it, you can see something in the left-hand corner
a thing that is like a branch: part of a tree
(balsam or spruce) emerging
and, to the right, halfway up
what ought to be a gentle
slope, a small frame house.

In the background there is a lake,
and beyond that, some low hills.

(The photograph was taken
the day after I drowned.

I am in the lake, in the centre
of the picture, just under the surface.

It is difficult to say where
precisely, or to say
how large or how small I am:
the effect of water
on light is a distortion.

but if you look long enough
eventually
you will see me.)

So . . . there I was, a nineteen-year-old man, an immigrant, listening to a Canadian woman read a poem that was crucial to him. "This Is a Photograph of Me" was not a "feminist" poem for me, not at the time. I didn't know, then, that feminism was important to Margaret Atwood, and it would not have occurred to me that feminism could pin down a poem's meaning. Nor did I read it as an encryption of my own "ghostly" situation. Being an immigrant and being black, I was, of course, aware that certain people are "seen," others not. But Atwood's poem didn't — or did not yet — have that kind of meaning for me. At the time, the things that mattered most as I listened to the poem were the house, the balsam (or spruce), the lake, and the low hills. The land is what mattered.

(Well, the land *and* Margaret Atwood's monotonous and suggestive voice.)

"This Is a Photograph of Me" held within itself a place and an anxiety — a ghost story, even — that corresponded to my own anxieties about being lost (or being gone) in Canada. Another way of putting it is: I thought I could recognize the vantage from which "This Is a Photograph of Me" was written, the *point* from which it was written. Atwood seemed conscious of the environment, the way a cautious animal is: uncertain of what's before her and what is not.

Interestingly, "This Is a Photograph of Me" echoes another poem that fascinated me in 1976, my first year at Carleton: Wallace Stevens's "The Snow Man." "The Snow Man" is more philosophically angular than Atwood's poem, but it preceded her to an intriguing place, a place where world and mind interact in singular ways. "The Snow Man" is a poem that (memorably) suggests there is such a thing as a "mind of winter" (intelligence or imagination as the essence of a season) and that one can hear "the sound of the land." More: both "This Is a Photograph of Me" and "The Snow Man" end with a listener (Stevens) or observer

(Atwood) who is both there and not there. Here is the "The Snow Man":

> One must have a mind of winter
> To regard the frost and the boughs
> Of the pine-trees crusted with snow;
>
> And have been cold a long time
> To behold the junipers shagged with ice,
> The spruces rough in the distant glitter
>
> Of the January sun; and not to think
> Of any misery in the sound of the wind,
> In the sound of a few leaves,
>
> Which is the sound of the land
> Full of the same wind
> That is blowing in the same bare place
>
> For the listener, who listens in the snow,
> And, nothing himself, beholds
> Nothing that is not there and the nothing that is.

When I first read Stevens's poem, it struck me as *Canadian*, and that provoked an interesting question: is it possible to write a "Canadian" poem without actually being Canadian? Could Wallace Stevens, an American poet, have been, unbeknownst to himself, secretly Canadian? As absurd as that question is, it has intrigued me for some time.

Partly as the result of that question, I conceived — when I was at Carleton — the idea of writing work that only Canadians could understand. Yes, I know: ridiculous, like a dog whistle for Canadians. But as someone who was unsure (and anxious about) what "Canadian" meant, it was, perhaps, natural for me to imagine a quality, an intellectual or emotional *aspect* shared by all who are Canadian, some quality I possessed, perhaps without being consciously aware of it, that was proof of my belonging. From there, it was a short step to imagining a literary work that could play on this quality or aspect I assumed all Canadians possessed.

Since then, I've come to think that the desire to write a short story or novel that could be understood only by Canadians is unworthy of a serious writer. A work which could only be understood by Canadians would have *military* value — you read it to someone at a border and discover at once if he or she is Canadian — but little else, excluding as it does most of humanity from its audience.

Or am I wrong here? I've come to accept that the greatest art is, inevitably, effortlessly universal, that great art triggers responses in readers irrespective of the reader's time and place. *The Iliad*, *War and Peace*, *King Lear* . . . these were all written *from* somewhere, and that *somewhere* is held within them. But, of course, it's not necessary to be Greek to understand *The Iliad* or English to understand *Lear*. Right. Fine. But what if, for argument's sake, the poem that could be understood only by Canadians were deeply *moving* to Canadians, a poem that called to their minds precisely the land from which they think, from which their selves derive their being? When I first imagined this work, I did not think of it as a Canadian epic, an *Iliad* set in Kapuskasing, for instance. Rather I imagined something like the distillation of a Canadian night, a distillate of time or moments or things experienced in Canada alone.[18]

---

18   In the documentary called *Ingmar Bergman on Life and Work*, Ingmar Bergman speaks with some wonder of the fact that he could still accurately visualize a room in his maternal grandmother's home. In that part of the film called "Dialogue with Childhood," Bergman says, ". . . my mother's mother died when I was twelve and I hadn't been [to her home] since I was maybe ten or eleven. And yet I can remember it in detail. There were things in that apartment that still have a magic significance and importance. I used a lot of that in *Fanny and Alexander*. If one can draw any conclusions from it . . . it may well be that, in a way, the whole of my creativity is in reality terribly childish. It's rooted in my childhood. I can, in less than a second, go right back into my childhood. I think that all I've done on the whole, anything of any value, has its roots in *my* childhood. Or, in dialectical terms, it's a dialogue with my childhood. I've never distanced myself from my childhood, but I have indeed carried on a dialogue with it. . . ." I've quoted Bergman at length, here, not because I identify with what he says, though I very much do, but because the "dialectic" Bergman describes brings to mind the dialectic I have with

I have abandoned most of the literary fantasies my nineteen-year-old self conceived. They were based on the longing to belong, longing for a quality I might acquire — or unknowingly possess — that would allow me to feel I could not be bereft of Canadian culture, or of the land that is Canada. No such quality exists, but the desire to find it still moves me at times.

And as I'm going to be your guide through certain scenes and a handful of Canadian works, it's probably good to know that your docent is, among other things, often troubled by desire for a "home."

My First Experiences in Toronto

I left Ottawa, in 1987, to accompany my then partner to Toronto, where she would go to the Ontario College of Art and I could become part of "literary society." I thought it might be good to meet Margaret Atwood or Michael Ondaatje, and I assumed they — and others I

---

the idea of "Canada." It is different, of course. "Canada" is a vivid, primal whiteness that influences the impressions, colours, and feelings in my daily life. When I say "whiteness," I mean that my country is in constant need of definition. It is always as it was when I first encountered it, at the age of four: mysterious, anxiety inducing. My daily experience brings me closer to an understanding of Canada, but paradoxically "Canada" is erased by my experience. Meaning: my country is not limited to my experience, is much greater than my experience of it, but my experience is crucial to an understanding of my country. A perverse dialectic, at the extremes of which either I or Canada is erased. That sounds excessively Hegelian, but the back and forth is crucial to my understanding of myself and of the land on which I dwell. And all of my writing has been part of this dialogue with my Canada.

admired — would recognize me as one of them: that is, as a writer.[19] (This is, of course, the worst possible reason to meet anyone.)

I had begun to write seriously in Ottawa. I had friends who were writers. One of them, Michael McCadden, had published a story in the *Malahat Review* and he'd had a play staged. That was success, as far as I was concerned. But one rarely heard about Ottawa writers in the forums that mattered to me: the *Globe and Mail*, *Canadian Fiction Magazine*, and so on. Well, no, you would *occasionally* read about Norman Levine, the one unquestionably great writer from Ottawa, but he hadn't lived in Ottawa for years, so his wasn't a living presence.[20]

---

19 I wanted to meet Ondaatje because I liked his poetry and had been overwhelmed by *Coming Through Slaughter*, which I'd read at one sitting, as if it were good mystery. Also, a friend of mine had once described going to a public reading at which Ondaatje had been one of the readers. Ondaatje, apparently, had been dressed in black and looked the part of a poet: moody, handsome, and slightly louche. He was, in a word, everything I wanted to be. When I did meet him, some ten years after coming to Toronto, I found him sympathetic, generous, not at all disappointing, but guarded. The kind of man who speaks more easily of what's going on with *you* than what's going on with him. Atwood: a different story. When I finally met her, Atwood seemed the embodiment not of the poetic but of the professional, a writer aware of herself as a writer, not unfriendly, not particularly friendly, either. On one occasion, she commiserated with me on the writing of my second novel. On another, she stuck her tongue out at me from across a table.

20 At the time I left Ottawa, I couldn't have told you why this "living presence" mattered. One *instinctively* seeks out those who have lived the life one wants to live. But then, in 2007, I was teaching at the University of

Toronto had something else going for it. Like any big city, it attracts writers from all over the country — all those who are ambitious, as I then was. I imagined I would meet the men and women who were my contemporaries, the ones engaged in the work I had devoted myself to doing: writing stories or plays or novels that mattered. (By "mattered," I mean I imagined myself and my contemporaries writing as well and as profoundly as Tolstoy or Joyce — unrealistic, because one has to be dead to be "Tolstoy" or "Joyce.")

Twenty-three years later, it seems I was both right and wrong to come to Toronto.

For me, at least, Toronto is a leveller. It has taken as much as it has given. An anecdote: during my first week in Toronto, I was looking for work. I was near the corner of Yonge and Bloor, a little south of Bloor, when I decided to cross the street from the east side to the west. The cars were stopped at the light. So, no danger.

Toronto and invited P. K. Page to speak to my creative writing class. She was a revelation. Not only a poet I had admired for some time, but the embodiment of a life lived in writing. It's hard to express what this "embodiment" means, exactly. P. K. didn't give the best answers I've heard to the questions she was asked. She gave *her* answers. But, in so doing, you could feel the depth of thought and feeling that had gone into the creation of her self and her work. My students were inspired by her. Against my own expectations, I was, too. By then, I had met any number of writers. But I felt, meeting P. K. Page, the cost and value of a life spent allowing the world to come through oneself in language and images. I could feel the nobility of her surrender to the process, and it renewed my own commitment to what is, in the end, a spiritual exercise.

But as I was about to step up onto the sidewalk, I noticed a disturbed-looking man with red "Dr. Zorba" hair coming at me. I paid no attention to him until he lowered his shoulder and knocked me back into the street. I didn't fall, but I was pushed back onto the road into the path of the cars that were now approaching. I stepped up onto the pavement, too stunned to do or think anything. And by the time I felt outrage, the incident was over. It felt as if the city were trying to tell me something, and I regretted moving from Ottawa. I'd have felt this way for some time if, almost immediately after the incident, I hadn't got my first job in Toronto, working in a bookstore. Rejection followed by acceptance: the pattern has defined my time in Toronto. It's as if the city and I are in love but don't actually like each other.

I was right to come to Toronto, in that I found the literary society and life I was looking for. I was wrong, in that I gradually discovered that the *last* thing I truly want is "literary society," and that the friendship of other writers can be a poisonous distraction. But, to deal with the good things first . . .

I came to the city at what was, I now see, a very good time for writers. It was 1987. Canadian writers were held in some regard, the world over. Still writing were Mordecai Richler, Margaret Atwood, Alice Munro, Mavis Gallant, Michael Ondaatje, Robertson

Davies, Al Purdy, Margaret Avison, Dennis Lee, Austin Clarke, bpNichol, The Four Horsemen, Timothy Findley, and even W. O. Mitchell. With the exception of Mavis Gallant, who lived in Paris and was a Montreal writer, all of them had some connection to Toronto.

The smaller presses, like Coach House, Mercury, or Anansi, were active and publishing challenging and, sometimes, very good work. There were elegant chapbooks done by marginal writers, by interesting writers, by all manner of writers. McClelland & Stewart was run by Jack McClelland, a very odd man — or so it seemed from the outside — who was, sadly, the last of the interesting publishers, a man whose personality was an unavoidable aspect — for good or bad — of his publishing house. More than that: Canadians were interested in their own writers.

My contemporaries, those who had just or would soon publish books that meant something to me, included Greg Hollingshead, Roo Borson, Don McKay, Nino Ricci, Linda Svendsen, Lynn Crosbie, Christian Bök, Shyam Selvadurai, Russell Smith, Michael Helm, Yann Martel . . . the list is long. And quite a number of these writers lived in or were connected to Toronto in some way as well. Toronto was flourishing.

Here's how my first book was published: I was working at Edwards Books and Art on Queen Street. My manager, Chris Mitchell, asked if I wanted to go with him to an open reading at Café May on Roncesvalles. Chris was going to read. He knew I was writing and he convinced me to come with him. Among the dozen or so reading that night, besides Chris and myself, were Michael Redhill, Russell Smith, and Eddy Yanovsky. I read a short piece, maybe two. People seemed appreciative. And that was that. My first public reading in Toronto.

Some time later, I was walking along Bloor Street, not far from Book City, where I now worked, carrying with me four short stories I'd photocopied at Kinko's. I had just stepped out of Kinko's when Michael Redhill (who'd heard me at Café May) greeted me. We talked for a few minutes. He asked if what I had in my hand were stories. I said "yes." He asked if he could read them, as he was on the editorial board at Coach House Press. I said "yes." Not long afterward, Michael called to ask if I had any more stories, enough to make a collection. I said "yes," though I didn't have any. I wrote four more stories. Redhill submitted them to the editorial board of Coach House Press, where they were seconded by Lynn Crosbie and Leon Rooke (for both of whom I still feel undying gratitude).

A year later, I held a copy of my first book, *Despair and Other Stories of Ottawa*, the original — still striking — cover done by Linda Watson, the woman with whom / for whom I'd come to Toronto.

And that's it.

(I wonder if this story is possible, twenty-three years on? The publishing industry, which was at its most optimistic in the late eighties, has become almost entirely pessimistic. Decisions made by editors enthusiastic about manuscripts are, these days, second-guessed — or disallowed — by marketing departments. Young writers will, no doubt, have less trouble in these times than writers who carry around with them chequered publishing histories. Marketing departments depend on track records to make their assessments. A new writer represents unknown potential. So, perhaps times are still good for new voices. Twenty years on, mine is no longer a "new voice," and I understand what it means to drag around the corpse of a previous book.)

Looking over the list of my contemporaries (Greg Hollingshead, et al.), it occurs to me there are very few whom I have not met. Some of those encounters have enriched my creative and intellectual life. But after a while, meeting writers is a lot like meeting *any* kind of petitioner: dull, unless you're really interested in their wares. And even then . . . Naturally, I'm not at all immune from this dullness. I don't think myself more interesting than my peers. I am as they are. (Perhaps I'm more aware of our relative dullness because I've worked in the theatre, where there are actors. Actors are as sensitive as writers, but they're almost all extroverts. So, they are good company, the way a happy, drunken man with a sharp stick is good company.)

Worse, literary society — the world of grudges, launches, and festivals — is *anti*-literary in a surprising way. First, there is the petty gossip and the secret enmities. Here, it would be easy to point out the pettiness of others, but I'd like to admit to my own enmities. There are a number of my fellow writers whom I loathe.[21] And, just so we understand each other, I'm not proud of my feelings. In fact, I'm dismayed to confront my dislikes, dismayed that I can feel loathing at all, now I'm in my fifties, a time by which, unless I was misinformed, I should have acquired at least some wisdom.[22] What is *anti*-literary about the loathing I

---

21   I would very much like to name these people. It feels cowardly to admit the feeling without delving, even if lightly, into it. After all, the writers I dislike are part of what drives my creativity. The reason I've chosen not to name these people is, first, that I can't stand to write their names. And then again, it distresses me to admit that the worst of me is such an integral part of the "spiritual exercise" that is writing.

22   When I was younger, I was obsessed with Russian literature. Tolstoy was my favourite, but the Dostoyevsky of *Brothers Karamazov* and the Turgenyev of *Fathers and Sons* weren't far behind. So, when I first read about Tolstoy's dislike of Turgenyev and his unwillingness to hang around St. Petersburg with the literary society of his time, I really couldn't understand it. Who *wouldn't* want to hang out with Dostoyevsky? I wondered. As it happens, Dostoyevsky and Turgenyev and Fet and whoever . . . most of them felt the same way. Once they'd found the vantage from which they would do their life's work, literary society became superfluous. Sadly, because it is the last nail in the coffin of my literary idealism, I now understand *exactly* why one wouldn't want to hang out with Fyodor or Ivan, Afanasy or Anton. One day, while I was talking to Michael Helm,

feel is that it keeps me, in one instance, at least, from reading work that is demonstrably good. Demonstrable by me, I mean, despite my dislike for the writer.

The second "anti-literary" aspect of literary society is related to the first. When I came to Toronto, along with the desire to meet those I admired, I had a longing for exchange. I imagined there would be endless, public talk about literature, about Tolstoy, Beckett, Raymond Queneau. I imagined I would be introduced to worlds of work I had missed. I imagined that the level of common discourse would be higher than it was in Ottawa. This wasn't the case, not at all. I have had interesting literary conversations with a handful of my contemporaries. (The number would be even smaller if I hadn't had two long-term relationships with writers, Catherine Bush and K,[23] both of whom are tremendously articulate.) As for the rest of my peers: we meet at launches, we say

---

he turned to me and said, "You know, other writers are a lot like family. You're glad they're alive, but you don't actually want to be around them too much." If you've been around writers for long enough, this will seem self-evident.

23   While Catherine did not mind my using her name, K very much did. So, it feels as if there are "black spots" in the text, places where others have pasted over parts of the window. While writing fiction, *I* choose those spots. *I* control what is revealed, in the name of a kind of "truth," which is, of course, a kind of lie. (Cocteau says of the poet, "I am a lie that tells only the truth." Not bad as a definition of fiction, either.) Though I understand perfectly why privacy is important, it is still a little odd to have those black spots determined by others. It is baffling, in fact, because in this essay I am as helpless before the (entirely reasonable) needs of others as I usually am before my own.

"hi," and we part. Maybe, before parting, we talk about Richard Ford spitting on Colson Whitehead or Evelyn Lau writing about the sagging, sallow flesh of W. P. Kinsella. The interesting exchanges about language and art, if they happened at all, happened in other parts of the room, among other writers.

On the other hand . . . why should one expect that people who'd spent their days writing and thinking would want to go out and *talk* about writing and thinking? The passion needed to talk about sentence structure in the work of Franz Kafka is something you tend to lose when you're actually writing your own work, isn't it? So, again, I was hopelessly naïve when I first came to the city and, perverse as it sounds, I hold my own naivety against Toronto itself, as if the city were responsible for my delusions.

My Peers (and More)

That previous section may make it seem as if I were bitter about my peers, as if most of what I've felt were dislike or disappointment. That's not true, though. My peers have also, at times, given me exactly what I was hoping for: friendship centred on our mutual love for language and work.

In any case, the intermingling of the personal and the literary has been almost unavoidable. By accident rather than design, *most* of my friends are or have been writers. And despite my disillusionment with the world around writing, despite my occasional desire to be something other than a writer, there are moments and encounters with my peers that have brought great solace and encouragement.

1. Tarragon Theatre Playwrights Unit (1989–1990)

The Playwrights Unit was created by Urjo Kareda, the artistic director of the Tarragon. It was, when I was invited to be a member, a weekly meeting of six would-be playwrights, writers Urjo thought talented or at least schoolable. We would sit around a long table and read work we had written. The object, though there was no great pressure to attain it, was to write a play in the year we spent together. Around the table with the members of the unit were Urjo himself (grossly over-weight, quiet, slightly skeptical, perceptive, thought-ful, not warm, a little forbidding but generous) and the Tarragon's assistant artistic director Andy McKim (warm, open with his opinions, steeped in theatre practice, the one who made me feel as if I had a place, the one with whom I could talk about practical mat-ters, the one who made me think I could be a play-wright if I wanted). Also with us around the table were playwrights who were in residence at the Tarragon. In 1989, that included Don Hannah, Ken Garnhum, Joan MacLeod, and Daniel MacIvor, though MacIvor, it was rumoured, was unhappy at the Tarragon and we saw little of him.

In 1989, the unit members included four men and two women. We were all around the same age, but we had very different sensibilities. As a result, I felt no competitive feelings at all. My closest friend in the unit, James O'Reilley, wrote things in a way that was much more emotionally raw than I could have. For that reason, he was probably the most influential on how I came to think about theatre. I had gone in thinking "Theatre" meant Samuel Beckett, inner experience made manifest. I also liked Pinter, Brecht, Wallace Shawn, and Arthur Kopit. O'Reilley wasn't like any of them. His monologues were a matter of catching his anger, frustration, and sense of humour in a way that suited his own performance style.

My most vivid memory of the 1989 Playwrights Unit has to do with helping O'Reilley memorize the lines of a play he'd written. He was living on Olive Avenue, I think it was. We had been accepted as part of the first — or was it the second? — Toronto Fringe Festival. We'd bought an hour's time and both of us had written short plays. Mine was called *Home*. It was not good. (As far as I know, I've destroyed all copies of the script.) O'Reilley's was called *Rude Circus*, a short monologue that would, with two other monologues, make up a play called *Work*. It was good, but he needed someone with whom to run lines. Walking in and around the Annex, O'Reilley speaking the lines of his play, me checking what he said against his script, was like sounding Toronto into a more solid existence. Those parts of the city where we walked exist within me accompanied by the *sound* — more than the words — of *Rude Circus*.

The other vivid memory I have of the time is also associated with the Fringe. My poor play was acted by David Jansen and David Collins. And it was Jansen who explained to me the connection between his body and memory. For him, perhaps for many actors, the words come back when his body is in the "right" position. Having worked out the blocking with the director — in this case, Colin Taylor — he would know that *this* word or phrase was associated with his body being in *this* position or *that*. His body remembered words. This was a revelation for me, a writer, because words come out when I am sitting down or lying down, not particularly aware of my body. In fact, my body is, to an extent, though not completely, the thing from which my mind drifts, writing being a form of untethering. So, it was profound, for me, to see Jansen at work and understand that *here* words were in the process of a grounding, a coming back to the body, and that acting is like writing but in reverse.

2. *K*

I have been in love with two writers in my life: K and Catherine Bush. The relationships, both of which have ended, were affectionate, and for me their endings were traumatic. In this, they were, I think, like all long-term relationships.

I am sometimes asked what it was like to live with — or go out with — other writers, the most common question being about influence: "Does your partner influence your work?" But it isn't a simple matter of direct influence, though there *is* direct influence as well. Rather, the two of you form a kind of third writer or third literary consciousness, one whose likes and dislikes are broader than either of yours and whose ideas are sometimes more surprising. The consciousness that is this "third writer" has its own life and curiosity. So, I would say, yes, I was influenced by both Catherine and K, but the deeper, more lasting influence was from this "third writer" ("Cath-André," in one case, "K-André" in the other) who went to places neither of us could go on his or her own.

I met K at a party at Barry Callaghan's home. I can't remember much about the party. Austin Clarke — a man who has been unfailingly encouraging to me — was there. I didn't speak much to anybody. And then Callaghan introduced me to someone he thought

I should meet, a young writer. She was wearing a buck-skin jacket and blue jeans. We talked, K and I, about small things. It was slightly awkward, I remember, until we talked about Banff. She had been there more recently than I, and in those days the writing colony at Banff was vibrant and interesting, a place where you could share intense literary moments with other writers or artists. (Some also shared sexual moments, of course. Something about Banff and the common pursuit of an art leads to a certain concupiscence, I guess. But the only time anyone tried to seduce me at Banff, I happened to be in love. The woman invited me back to her cabin in the Leighton Colony, brought out a bottle of champagne, and then grew progressively bored as I drank and droned on about the woman with whom I was infatuated.)

Our memories of Banff kept us talking for a while, and then we drifted apart and somewhat avoided each other as we went into or out of Callaghan's house. When it was late, too late to take a subway, K and I were in the kitchen together and I volunteered to walk with her, as our houses were in the same direction. We walked for an hour and a half, I guess, and talked about writing and ritual and the meaning of the sacred. We argued, actually, but the night wasn't cold or the morning wasn't cold and I felt, as we walked together, an intense closeness.

A curiously prophetic detail: near the corner of Bloor and Christie, where we stopped to go on talking, a man was lying in a restaurant doorway. He asked us if we had cigarettes and then asked for a light. He then lay down on the pavement as if he were on a sofa and looked up at us as if we were his friends. He wanted to join our conversation, but he was clearly stoned and, besides, I was wary. On the night I'd met my *previous* partner, we were walking along Harbord when, near the Innes library, a man on a bicycle rode over to our side of the street and shouted at us "I fucking hate heterosexuals!" as he rode off. It was startling, and it's hard not to take an incident like that as a portent of something or other. So, with K, near the corner of Bloor and Christie, I wanted to get away from the man as quickly as possible, worried as I was about what his interruption might presage.

Unfortunately, he was the harbinger of an even bigger interruption. My novel *Childhood* was published just after K and I began seeing each other and it broke the spine of our relationship. Still, our first two years had an effect on how I thought about writing, on what I wanted to write. I knew more about literature than K did, but she knew more about psychology, and it was through her that I first learned about John Bowlby (his *Attachment and Loss* is a trilogy of books about how humans come to intimacy and how they deal with bereavement) and D. W. Winnicott (the psychologist who first theorized about "transitional objects").

Also, K wasn't quite a poet, as yet. She'd written a novel and a collection of stories. But poetry was already on her horizon in a way that it was not on mine. I first read Don McKay's *Night Field* at her house, and one evening we spent an hour together, lying in bed reading and rereading "Tulips" by Sylvia Plath, comparing it to a poem by Tess Gallagher which, after a couple of readings, ceased to seem like the real thing. "Tulips" was so clearly the stronger poem that we gave ourselves over to trying to understand how it worked: counting syllables, thinking about its repetitions of *ee* ("gently," "sleep," "me," "breathe," "baby," etc.) and feeling where the poem turns strange for good with the line

The tulips are too red in the first place, they hurt me.

It was an hour during which we were like two children before a magic show whose trickery we imagined we could, together, sort out. In the end, Plath's art isn't circumscribable in an hour. But we were left with the pleasure of having made a voyage into the poem together.

3. Catherine

I can't remember how Catherine and I met. Almost certainly, it was through her then-partner Nigel Hunt, another writer, a man I like very much, especially since he helped me to walk back to the theatre, on my play's (*Lambton Kent*) opening night, after I had been drinking.

Long after Catherine and Nigel's relationship had ended, I was invited by Catherine to give a reading in her class in Montreal. From that time on, we were friendly. Then, after a while, our friendship became intimacy.

All of our time passed under the aegis of literature. It was perhaps significant that, during our first year together, we were invited to the Santa Maddalena Retreat for Writers and Botanists, a writers' retreat run by Baronessa Beatrice Monti della Corte von Rezzori, the writer Gregor von Rezzori's widow. We stayed on one floor of a thirteenth-century Tuscan tower, with Zadie Smith having the floor above us to herself (or to herself with bats). Catherine and I did nothing but write, eat, and, after suppers, talk with Zadie and Beatrice about Literature or Art.[24]

---

24 I remember quite a bit about our time at Santa Maddalena. Beatrice was a fantastically generous European snob. She had owned an art gallery in Milan and had once spent a day in Athens (I think it was) with Marcel Duchamp. Zadie was friendly and entirely unpretentious. There were a handful of visitors during my month at Santa Maddalena: Alexander Chancellor, Alexander Waugh and his wife, and Colm Tóibín. What I remember most vividly, though, is the groundskeeper, an Algerian or Middle Eastern man: short, thin as a whippet. He was in his thirties, I

After our time at Santa Maddalena, we spent a month in Positano in a home belonging to the friends of friends. We spent the month writing together. That is, in proximity. We would get up in the morning, go down the 122 steps to the beach, and swim in the Mediterranean. After that, breakfast. And after breakfast, we would write: Catherine in the living room (*Claire's Head*), me at a table in the kitchen (*Asylum*). Once the writing day was over, when the sun had gone down, we would water the garden or explore Positano or read, with one of us eventually cooking supper.

I'm writing about our time in Italy because although it was not entirely happy, there were transcendent moments. One evening in particular, after a day of

---

guess, very friendly to me, but with a wary and slightly pugnacious look on his face at all times. He and his wife cooked, cleaned, and did what menial work needed to be done. Unfortunately, the Algerian man was a bit of a know-it-all. Before we had come, the chickens Beatrice kept for their eggs had developed a strong case of fleas. Rather than bring in a vet and waste the Baronessa's money, the Algerian decided to deal with the problem himself. Convinced that it was the chickens' anuses that were the problem, that their anuses attracted the fleas, he took a cotton swab rubbed with DDT and, daily, cleaned the chickens' anuses. He didn't tell anyone that he'd decided to do this. He simply went ahead with it. Not surprisingly, the chickens began to die out. No one could figure out why, until they discovered what the Algerian had done and understood that the chickens were dying from DDT poisoning. This story itself suggests the odd irreality of Santa Maddalena. The other thing I vividly remember is Santa Maddalena's guest book. It was signed by a number of artists and writers. The signature I remember best was by Robert Wilson, the theatre director. It was so appealing to me, I tried to write my own name in Wilson's style for some time afterwards.

writing, we lay in the bedroom together and Catherine read to me from her novel. In the same way that reading Plath's "Tulips" was confirmation of how deeply I could be affected by poetry, this was a revelation. I listened as a fellow writer allowed me into *her* world of words. I can remember the bedroom still: white walls, bed on the ground, bathroom off to one side, a window facing the sea in one direction and the side of a mountain in the other. (At night, the constellations were so clear, it was easy to name the zodiac as it moved across the sky.) It was hot. We lay on top of the covers, me on my stomach, Catherine sitting up with her back against the wall. And I heard the latest version of the beginning to *Claire's Head*.

I miss being so close to someone else's creativity, the thousands and thousands of micro-level decisions that go into writing a novel. Catherine's work's imperfections and possibilities were a mirror of the imperfections and possibilities in my own early drafts.

It's a paradox I haven't quite thought through, but this moment with Catherine, a moment during which I felt privileged to be the first to hear a fellow writer's work, was also the beginning of the end of my caring about "literary society." When we went back to Toronto, I began to feel more and more distant from the writing community. And in fact, our time together in Positano (reading Catherine's novel or translating Italo Calvino's *Il visconte dimezzato* together, word for word, the listener holding the dictionary while the reader sounded the words out) was the last time I was completely happy to be a writer.[25]

4. K (2)

Ten years after we broke up, K and I began to see each other again. By this time, she was a committed poet, a member of a poetry reading group that included writers whose work I respect, like Maureen Hynes and Barry Dempster. Her ideas about poetry were fully developed and, now, radically different from mine.

Our differences were thrown into relief when Jacob Scheire won a Governor General's Award for Poetry. K didn't feel he *deserved* the award, but she defended his poetry, while I couldn't find anything in it to defend. The crux of the matter was, for me, Scheier's unmemorable language and the slackness of his verse. For K, the poetry dealt with palpably *true* emotion. It wasn't formless, and some of his lines and line breaks were subtle and created interesting wordplay. I saw some of her point and came to think of Scheier's poetry less harshly.

The thing about this second K, so very different from the first, was that she brought poetry into my life directly. With her, I began to seriously think about

---

25   So, the last time I was entirely happy to be a writer was, in fact, when I was most a *reader*.

what poetry is, what it was meant to do, how it did what it did. Though I have always loved it, I had never thought to write poetry myself or, rather, I *did* think to do it, but I was so self-conscious about the writing that it destroyed whatever I wrote. With this second K — *for* her, rather — I surrendered to the idea of writing poetry. I wrote, with her in mind, the only poetry I have ever allowed myself to nurture; meaning: I went as far as I could with the poems I wrote, treating them seriously before setting them aside — not abandoned, as I had abandoned all the previous poetry I'd written, but left aside waiting for a (possible) moment of completion or a moment of resigned defeat.

Maybe the most important aspect of this, for me, is that the writing of poetry has brought me back to *zero*, to the beginning of writing, unsure of what I'm doing, dependent on others to tell me what the work *feels* like to them, what it does. I'm once again an amateur.

To Washington D.C., August 16, 2008

These days, I think about a laconic
or taciturn life, life in need of Roman
words, words that end on the steps of the senate,
Caesar's life balanced against the needs of the people.
Flying over the green hills of Pennsylvania,

the land modest and strong, is not flying
over the ragged, earth-scoring settlements
that send up their own clouds, as if in defiance of God:
Pittsburgh, Philadelphia, Washington.
Do the same creatures inhabit such different grounds?
How to judge among the populi?
Who are they to be weighed against Caesar?
It would take a stoic, one who has reasoned
patiently, to know when to add his knife to those
of the conspirators or when to put
his own chest forward in defiance.
Coming in to land at Washington International,
Memorial Bridge looking like dangerous
lace over the Potomac, these questions rise
as in a flood. What a strange age we live in, an age lower
than Auden's, more casually base. Even
the prospect of change brings apprehension
for some further, new debasement.
Confusion and doubt bring with them thoughts about
the senator from Illinois: great, honest,
despicable or what? As the plane sinks into
D.C., I think again of Illinois, and of a word:
marble. Infinite marble. All potential,
like the roar of the plane's engines, all sound
and silence at once. Neither Caesar nor of the
people, not of his time nor far from it,

no conspirator, no altruist, either.

Coming in to land, I hear both everything

and nothing and wonder about America.[26]

Whether this poem is good or bad, indifferent or
promising, it is the product of a willingness to be vulnerable — because poetry, which leaves you little place

---

26   I could have chosen a less "finished" poem, here, I guess. In the
Beckett essay, I chose the awkward and ungainly, because the struggle
for emotion *and* for distance — for reconciliation — is what I was after.
It's what I'm after here, too, to an extent. But I've destroyed most of the
poems I wrote while I was with K. The only other one I might have chosen
I did not because a poet friend remarked that the final lines feature a
rhyme that was too dead on: "do," "you." It sounded to her like "moon" and
"June," and she suggested that John Donne, for instance, would have been
more subtle. In this, she was wrong. For comedic effect, John Donne does,
in fact, use common rhymes. In "Woman's Constancy," for instance, he
rhymes "could" and "would," "you" and "true," "do" and "too." But her point
had to do with something deeper. The poem was problematic because its
four final lines didn't deal with the emotion of its beginning.
    For a prose writer (for me, at any rate), the criticism of poets often has
to be interpreted with the same care one uses to interpret their poems.
The poets I know, aware as they are that the change of one word can alter
the meaning(s) of a poem, are hesitant in their suggestions. Their criti-
cisms are preceded by words like "It's your poem, so . . ." or "This is good,
if you're happy with it . . ." When writers of prose — professional writers,
I mean — criticize your work, they mention structure, characterization,
rhythm. They point to concrete "problems" in your novel or story. Their
comments are less cloud-like, less vague, though not necessarily better or
more helpful. Though it may not have as many words as a short story, a
poem can take longer to finish. So, in a way, poetic criticism can be like Zen
koans, aids to a meditation on poetry. Not that there aren't moments when
poets are entirely clear. After I sent him a poem in which I had compared
the body of a drowned goat floating in the Mediterranean to a "roving
footstool," Michael Redhill wrote: "Lose the fucking footstool. Just because
something looks like another doesn't make it a good image." A good lesson
for prose writers, too, but a matter of life and death for poets.

to hide, *does* make you vulnerable. And, in part, this willingness came out of my respect for the nakedness of K's work.[27] I said above that when one is living with another writer, the greatest influence comes from the "third writer" that the two of you create together. This is true, but no other writer, certainly none with whom I've had such combustible disagreements, has taught me more about my own aesthetic frailties — which is to say, more about myself, in the end.

But there's something else here.

I mean, why *should* I wish to be an amateur again? Why be vulnerable in poetry when I've spent years learning a discipline (prose) that I haven't yet mastered? What is there about humiliation and creation that they should go so closely hand in hand?[28]

I can't speak for other writers, of course. But, for me, the humiliation of beginning anew, feeling helpless, is very like the experience of coming to Canada for the first time. There is a fear of judgement, a waiting for disapproval, a humiliation in anticipation of humiliation. Rather than avoid this feeling, I have spent a lot of my creative life reliving it. It's a way to remember my

---

27   In the story "Cocteau," from the first section of this book, some of Marin's poetry was lifted (with permission) from K's work.

28   And not just for me, either. According to Philip Guston, a great painter, the artist Franz Kline once said to him: *"You know what creation really is? To have the capacity to be embarrassed."*

beginnings, yes, but also a way of saying "This doesn't hurt me," though of course it does. Being unsure of a poem, a play, a radio monologue — when trying to do those things for the first time — is embarrassing in exactly the way it was embarrassing to be asked to say words I would "mispronounce" in my Trinidadian accent when I first came to Canada. "Mastery" is also part of the mechanism. I felt I belonged, the day I was able to say "ask," not "aks," the day people stopped asking me to say things, because I had learned to say them in a way that no longer marked me as an outsider.

A Literary Culture in Decline

A sadness has dogged my time in Toronto. This is the city in which I have been disabused of a number of useless notions, where I have lost a certain innocence. I would have lost it in London or Paris, Tokyo or Port of Spain, no doubt. But my education has happened here, in Toronto, during this long decline in Canadian literary culture. So, my sadness is for the loss of innocence as well as for my culture's slow agony.

Where to start?

I am writing these words on January 1, 2010, almost exactly twenty-three years after I first came to Toronto. The *Toronto Star*'s book section is small, ineptly edited, and not worth reading. (And when I say "ineptly edited," I mean that the current book editor, in allowing personal attacks and collegiate vitriol to stand as "book reviews," has directly contributed to the irrelevance of the two measly, advert-ridden pages the *Star* now puts out, dutifully, Sunday after Sunday.) The *Globe and Mail*'s book section has been reduced from a stand-alone magazine to a handful of pages in the Focus section. The *Globe* book section's slow death has been even more painful to witness than the *Star*'s.[29]

Neither the *Sun* nor the *National Post* has a book section that is worthy of mention. *Eye* magazine, under Kevin Connolly's stewardship, was interesting, but it's been quite a while since Kevin was there and it's much less interesting now. *NOW* magazine's book page is, I think, unspeakably amateurish, and one wonders why they bother with books at all. One wonders why *any* of them bother. Is it to some feeling of guilt that we owe such book sections as remain, like vestigial limbs, in our newspapers?

In the eighties and early nineties, the *Globe and Mail*'s book section was very good indeed. Stan Persky — one of my favourite Canadian reviewers — wrote for the *Globe*, as did Jay Scott, though he was the paper's

---

29   I'm a contributing reviewer to the *Globe and Mail*'s book section, but I'm entirely pessimistic about the section's future. The book section's editor, Martin Levin, still manages to find capable reviewers, now and then, but one wonders if the newspaper itself really cares, since it has decided to pander to popular taste (or, more accurately, the *decline* in popular taste) by shortening the reviews and including breezy interviews with "interesting" authors.

film reviewer. (In fact, for a moment there, the intellectual aspirations of our reviewers was almost baffling. I remember being pleasantly stunned when Jay Scott spoke of Roland Barthes in the course of reviewing a Hollywood picture.) There were also Morris Wolfe and George Fetherling. The *Toronto Star* was almost as good, in those days. Ken Adachi was their regular reviewer, with Robert Fulford and Urjo Kareda, among others, contributing.

But why should the death of book review sections matter?

My answer to that question is entangled in my idealism. For me, book sections have been, even if only potentially, necessary forums for the exchange of ideas. When I read the *New York Review of Books* or the *Times Literary Supplement*, I can, if I choose, find out what John Searle thinks about relativism. I can read about Tariq Ali's or Ian Buruma's thoughts on Islam in Europe. I can revisit Galileo's relationship to the church or Stephen J. Gould's thoughts on baseball. Books are where ideas come to you without a middleman, but the reception books and ideas are given is matter from the agora, the place where men and women work out what it is they think about politics, religion, science, art, and beauty. In other words, a book section isn't only about letting people know that such and such a work has been published. It's a place where consideration happens, and the nature of a consideration is important, whatever book or idea sets it in motion. ("Consideration," for me, isn't so much a matter of determining the ultimate value of a work, but rather of allowing a community to participate in the evaluation of the work.) I also think that book review sections, being public and relatively slow-moving—being *moderated*—are superior to blogs, which descend into squabbling—and the desire to dominate—well before proper consideration has been given to the ideas under discussion. The anonymity of online commentary is counter-agoran. Not knowing with whom you're dealing means not knowing where you are.

Not to go too deeply into the obvious but, of course, there are any number of *agorai*. The audience for the *New York Review of Books* (leftist) is not identical to that for the *Times Literary Supplement* (rightist). A good book review section (or, as is the case with the *New York Review of Books*, a magazine) gives us a strong picture of a particular agora. The *Globe and Mail*'s book section as it was in the eighties was an inspiring venue for Canadian intellectual life, one that allowed me to believe in the seriousness of my fellow countrymen.

So, in answer to my own question: for me, the loss or decline of book sections has been part of the loss or decline of my community.

There is a second part to this answer, though . . .

These days, Canadian literary reviewing is so woefully incompetent, it makes you wonder if there's something in our culture that poisons critics in their cradles. I was once told, by a short, pompous man with thick, dark-rimmed glasses (a self-styled "critic"), that criticism is "the rich loam out of which literature blooms." If that were the case, Canadian literature would have withered, died, and blown away long ago. The failure of our country to produce a single literary critic of any worth, at least since the death of Northrop Frye, is striking. And in this age when book review pages are disappearing from our dying newspapers, things are likely to get worse. That is, we're likely to be left with nothing but the sheer opinion-spreading that passes for critical thought these days.

How we got to this pass is difficult to articulate. Or, rather, there are such a number of interesting narratives, it's difficult to settle on any single one. Is Canadian literary reviewing worse than British or American reviewing? In that there is less of it, yes. In that there are fewer venues for it, yes. But neither the British nor the Americans have produced any particularly compelling critics lately, either. James Wood, who is the one name anyone mentions — and there is a kind of desperation in the mentioning — is, by his own choice, a limited critic. His assumption is that his judgement — a decision on whether or not such and such a work is "good" — is the most important aspect of "criticism" has led to lively enough talk, but he has not, as far as I know, written a convincing work to elucidate what it is we do when we write fiction or provided a *new* vantage from which to look on literature.[30] In his way, Wood is a throwback

---

30 In an article on Henry James, Wood wrote, "contemporary scholars are simply not interested in value judgment at all (they have smaller fish to fry)." James Wood is interested in value judgements. He takes them as a chief part of his intellectual brief. In a review of Denis Donoghue's *Speaking of Beauty*, he reuses the "smaller fish to fry" analogy and then says "Who bothers, when teaching *Portrait of a Lady* for the umpteenth time, to explain that it is a great book and a beautiful one?" Now, surely the job is to explain *why* the book is "great" or "beautiful," not *that* it is "great" or "beautiful." And in explaining *why*, academics — for whom Wood, here, has little but scorn and derision — do resort to showing *how* the book achieves its effects. Is there a more efficient way to demonstrate "greatness" or "beauty"? At the beginning of his career, James Wood sought to make a virtue — perhaps the ultimate virtue — of the reviewer's *declaration* of what is great and what beautiful.

Now, my words about Wood's critical thinking concern *The Broken Estate*, his first book, above all, and such practical criticism of his as I've chanced to read in *The New Yorker* or in other places over the last few years. (His latest book, *How Fiction Works*, is a different kettle of fish. It marks the beginning of an interesting critical endeavour. And it warrants separate consideration.) As far as I can tell, Wood's insights into fiction are really descriptions (of plot or language) and analogy, not the result of any particularly deep understanding. Here's another (and fairly typical) sentence from his essay on Henry James: "The particular difficulty, and the difficult reward, of late James is the way in which he transfers his own acute sensitivity to verbal calibration onto his characters: they become Chief Justices of the word, forever raising to moral scrutiny certain anointed terms and phrases. This is what gives late James its strongly philosophical flavor." These are, conspicuously, "writerly" sentences, a little overwrought for their purpose, because Wood is preening. And then, "Chief Justices of the word"? An interesting analogy, but what does it mean, and what does it mean when applied to Maisie or Mrs. Gereth? Is the difference between Daisy Miller (early James) and Maisie (late James), both of them "innocents," really down to Maisie being authoritatively sensitive to language? And is it his characters' Jamesian language use that gives late Henry James its "strongly philosophical flavour" or, more plausibly,

to practitioner/critics like Nabokov or Tolstoy whose judgements are part of their own aesthetic process, having more to do with how *they* create than with understanding the work under consideration. (Think, for instance, of Nabokov's schoolmarmish condescension towards Dostoyevsky, or Tolstoy's inability to see any value in Shakespeare's work.) Wood's inability to appreciate Paul Auster or Thomas Pynchon is in no way a victory for the critical — or, rather, reviewing — consciousness. It's a defeat. And part of what is wrong these days is the forgetting that there is such a thing as the defeat of the critic. Criticism is, by its nature, the chronicle of a small community: writer, book, reader.[31] It is, for the brief time it exists, a community of equals. A reader/critic who fails to appreciate or understand a book tends to blame the book or the writer. And, in fact, it may well be that book X is ineptly done or that the writer is at fault. But readers are generally blind to their own deficiencies and reviewers even more so. It's very, very rare to find a reviewer — whose job, after all,

---

the play of moral and philosophical ideas along with James's constant struggle for expository precision? For me, Wood's insights, in his earlier work, are almost inevitably flimsy and a product of his performative reviewing.

31   Better put, this sentence would read "*Reviewing* is, by its nature, the chronicle of a community. . . ." For the *reviewer*, the community is "writer, book, reader." For the critic, the community is much broader: writer, writer's predecessors, book, reader, reader's predecessors.

is to convince us that he or she knows whereof he or she speaks — who will even admit the possibility that he or she is the weak member in the community he or she is chronicling.

Well, yes, but what should the reviewer do? Begin every negative review with a *mea culpa*, an apology for his or her betrayal of the book under consideration? No, that's not necessary. The problem is, rather, in the approach. Our reviews have become, at their worst, about the revelation of the reviewer's *opinion*, not about a consideration of the book or an account of the small world that briefly held writer and reviewer in the orbit of a book. Reviews have turned into a species of *autobiography*, with the book under review being little more than a pretext for personal revelation.[32]

---

32 Reviewing is, *inevitably*, an exercise in personal revelation. The extent of and importance given to personal revelation are what's at issue. It sometimes feels as if *the* characteristic of our current reviewing culture is acceptance of the idea that the critical reading of a work of literature is an essentially antagonistic activity, and that "writer, reader, book" don't form a "community" so much as they do the boundaries of a battlefield. Martin Amis, in one of his least convincing moments, complained that fiction is the only art whose critics use the same genre (prose narrative) as its creators, thus creating a competition between author and reviewer. To Amis, a review is a prose narrative. (Clive James seconded Amis's opinion by suggesting that a person who writes a memorably witty review can demonstrate his or her literary superiority to the writer whose [unmemorable] work is being assessed.) The reason I think this unconvincing is that it is a surprising refusal to accept that a "prose narrative" is not any one *single* thing. Comparing the writing in a book review to the writing in a novel (even a bad novel) makes no more sense than comparing a travelling salesman joke (as much a "prose narrative" as a review) to Tolstoy's *War*

If I had to blame any one *Canadian* writer for this state of affairs, I'd blame John Metcalf.[33] I think Metcalf's influence on reviewing has been woeful and unfortunate. At least, it is if you accept my version of how we've come to the place we're at . . .

Northrop Frye was a great critic, but his work — and some of the work he influenced, Margaret Atwood's *Survival* above all — was one of the stimuli for a kind of populist critical rebellion. Frye's work was academic, specialized, and structuralist. *The Anatomy of Criticism* is a book that, it's been suggested, put methodology

---

and Peace. Their intentions, purposes, lifespan, and ground are all entirely different, so much so that to speak of a reviewer's competition with the writer because he or she uses the same means as a writer makes no sense without so much qualification that it comes down to asserting the obvious, that the same *physical* means used to write a novel — pen and paper or typewriter or word processor — may be used to write a review. There are no more grounds for "competition," here, than there are grounds for competition between nuts and bolts (on one hand) and a statue by Henry Moore (on the other) though all were fired in the same foundry. But what *is* interesting about Amis's contention is the palpable anxiety it demonstrates about the book reviewer's power and intentions. Amis is a book reviewer himself, and his ideas about the competitive relationship between a writer and a reviewer are, possibly, rooted in his own competitive feelings vis-à-vis the books (and writers) he himself judges.

33   It is, of course, *rhetorical* to blame any one person for attitudes that spread through a population. Metcalf is the purveyor of ideas that, at a certain time in our literary history, met with a certain approval. Most of Metcalf's successful ideas came not from him but from Kingsley Amis, Philip Larkin (see Larkin's "The Pleasure Principle," for instance), or the *British* writers he clearly admired. But it's hard to blame Larkin or Amis for ideas disseminated by Metcalf and treated with more seriousness here, in Canada, than they were in England, where Larkin and Amis were, rightly, treated as tendentious conservative codgers as often as not.

first and, to an extent, the literary works it was scrutinizing second. I don't think that's entirely fair. Frye's respect for the literary work was, to me, inspiring. And he was a good practical critic (or critical reviewer). He could write a clear evaluation of Wallace Stevens, say, that was accessible to all, whether you had read his *Anatomy of Criticism* or not.

Atwood's *Survival* was also academic and, perhaps, a little rigidly methodological. It put classification above aesthetic consideration. The works Atwood writes about are put into categories she has devised, their importance based on taxonomy. Personally, I think *Survival* is a brilliant book, suggestive and stimulating, but a common complaint of Metcalf's and of those influenced by him was that critics like Atwood rated books more highly than they should have because, for instance, they were examples of "Canadian Gothic." Books by, again for instance, Frederick Philip Grove which, practically speaking, had little real influence on Canadian writing were lauded because they were exemplars of certain tendencies in Canadian literature. To Metcalf, this meant that academics had created or were creating a distorted version of Canadian literature. Worse, academic classification — as an end in itself — gave the impression that academics are the ones best equipped to deal with literary works. Refusing to deal with whether a book was actually any good or not, refusing to *judge* a work's sheer aesthetic worth, led to a breach in the reading public. On one side, in their ivory towers, were the academics who never allowed themselves to be troubled by trivial things like the actual pleasure a book gives. On the other side were writers like John Metcalf who insisted that not only was the pleasure a book gave important, but that the pleasure it gave was, likely, a better indication of the book's influence as well. That is, people read and love *The Apprenticeship of Duddy Kravitz*. They don't read, unless forced to, *Settlers of the Marsh*. So, what does "influence" mean if you can call *Settlers of the Marsh* as influential a work as *Duddy Kravitz* simply because *Settlers* is an exemplar of the immigrant's tale?

In the 1980s, Metcalf waged an effective campaign against "academic" criticism. He cultivated and published writers who announced their allegiance to him by insisting that the pleasure a book gives is its most important aspect. In *Kicking against the Pricks*, which is by some distance his best book, I think, Metcalf makes a convincing case for his concerns. For one thing, in an essay called "Punctuation as Score," he demonstrates a sensitivity to language and he makes *that* something of a calling card. (It's as if he were saying: I've meditated on words, on what they can do, and on how they are most effectively used. Have you?) An essay like "Punctuation as Score" is, for me, at any rate, so amusing — and instructive — that it's possible to forgive the shaky foundation of his argument in other parts of the book. Foremost among the shaky arguments is the idea that "good writing" is easily distinguished from bad. Anyone who has actually tried to set down rules to help discriminate between good and bad writing knows just how difficult this is. Metcalf doesn't set down rules, though. He takes sentences or paragraphs that he considers examples of "brilliant" writing and then does the written equivalent of pointing and saying, "There, you see?" Having spent so much time arguing against the "academic," there really isn't much more that Metcalf *can* do. He has painted himself into a corner where any introduction of system or method would itself be considered "academic." Not surprisingly, Metcalf and his followers do a lot of pointing.

Another problem for those who wander into his critical books looking for help in finding "good writing" is that Metcalf tends to like "finicky" and he particularly likes *English* versions of "finicky." His own sentences, which he sometimes quotes as examples, are often overwritten and, at times, awkward in their frank desire to be good. It wouldn't, usually, be fair to point to the failings in a man's prose as a sign that he does not know good prose from bad. There are great critics who can recognize the good in art without being able to reproduce it themselves. But Metcalf is a special case. In a recent autobiographical book called *An Aesthetic Underground: A Literary Memoir*, he compares literature to fine wine and speaks of his sensibility as if it were a highly developed palate. He suggests that, as a connoisseur of wine can tell good wine from bad with a sip, so the trained literary mind can tell a good book after a page or two. *He* has made his sensibility the issue.

Now, of course, many critics behave this way. Metcalf himself borrowed the "connoisseur" analogy from Cyril Connolly. But a novel or short story is different from wine in that, often and with the best work, you must finish to know what is effective and what is not. It's easy to pick bad sentences in Poe's work (Aldous Huxley does and snickers at them). But Poe stays in the mind, awkward prose or not. (*Crome Yellow*? Not so much, though it is certainly "better written.") Dostoyevsky is a similar case. Yes, Nabokov was right to criticize Dostoyevsky's writing. And yes, *Demons* is, for long stretches, badly written and tedious. But I defy anyone to point to the equivalent, anywhere in world literature, of the scene in which Kirilov, the nihilist, must decide whether or not to kill himself. Pure, unforgettable nightmare. Fanatics of "great prose," like Metcalf (or Nabokov), reduce novels and stories to one of their elements and then insist that *that* element — style, in this case — is the legitimate one for critical consideration.

What Metcalf and Cyril Connolly before him have done is to declare the finesse of their own sensibilities sufficient to tell "good" work from "bad." But, of course, they are the only possessors of their sensibilities. There is no basis for a universal aesthetic scale, unless the thought behind a sensibility is unpacked. Just to be clear: I'm convinced that Metcalf and I, if we sat down together and read a page from such and such a book, would agree, maybe eight times out of ten, on what is good and what is not. On the evidence, I think Metcalf and I have similar sensibilities. But those who have been influenced by him — Ryan Bigge, for instance — don't possess the same credibility as Metcalf, though they allow themselves to make the same kinds of pronouncements.

So, one could legitimately say that Metcalf has turned a generation of critics away from "academic" evaluations of literature. He has insisted that pleasure is the most important aspect of any work (as Larkin did before him) and he made the critic's own pleasure (or non-pleasure) the accepted content in an evaluation of literary works. Finally, he has, in anthologies like *The Bumper Book*, encouraged reviewers to vividly express their opinions, especially their unfavourable opinions, in the belief that a vivid put-down, first, is more entertaining and, second, leads to "discussion."

For twenty years now, we've had the "discussions" that unfounded, pugnacious reviews bring. What knowledge or understanding have they given us? Ryan Bigge insulting Leah McLaren in the pages of the *Toronto Star*, Carmine Starnino insulting whoever doesn't happen to share his preference for certain kinds of verse, Philip Marchand expressing the opinion that poets shouldn't write novels, David Solway insisting that a perfectly understandable and well-crafted poem by Al Purdy is not good because *he* doesn't understand it. The discussion is rarely helpful in building a lucid aesthetic. One of the very few clear aesthetic opinions shed by Philip Marchand, for instance, is his belief that anyone who does not appreciate the greatness of Tolstoy's *War and Peace* is "simply deficient in taste." A dubious opinion, given that Henry James, who surely has as great a claim to "taste" as Marchand, and the later Tolstoy, who felt that *War and Peace* was badly done, both disliked the novel. As with all Metcalf's children — and all of the writers I've just mentioned have been edited or published by him — Marchand's statement is about himself, *his* belief in *War and Peace*'s greatness. He offers no defence of his opinion, believing that none is required. And so we have come to the point where the *fact* of an opinion is more important than the basis for it. As I suggested, this is neither criticism nor reviewing but autobiography. Marchand is telling me something about himself. Starnino is telling me about his sensibility and how much he believes in his beliefs. Bigge is settling a personal vendetta with McLaren. Solway is demonstrating the depths to which he'll stoop to belittle Al Purdy or Anne Carson or whomever it is he doesn't like this week.

We have gone so far away from the idea of criticism, from the elaboration of an aesthetic vision tested against the books we read, that it really doesn't matter who comments on our books or poems or plays. One opinion is as valuable as any other, because the work is a pretext for talk about oneself or for the generation of high emotion. If, under the supposed tyranny of academic criticism, the literary object disappeared under a mountain of methodology, nowadays it vanishes beneath the ego of the reviewer or the reviewer's desire to create "talking points."

So, this is Metcalf's progress: the discovery of a different road to the same desecration.

The magazine *Walrus* published a version of this section of "Water." They asked for an optimistic ending. So, I wrote this coda:

We move, as critical thinkers, towards the communal or away from it, towards the idea of a common critical enterprise or back to belief in the sanctity of opinion. So, perhaps the time has come to revisit the idea of literary theory, to reconsider a virtue at the heart of it.

In *Alternating Currents*, Octavio Paz writes of criticism that it is "a world of ideas that as it develops creates an *intellectual space*: a critical sphere surrounding a work of literature, an echo that prolongs it or contradicts it. Such a space represents the meeting place with other works, the possibility of a dialogue between them." Paz's is a vision of "criticism" as communal construct, the creation of a place where books meet, but it can also be taken as the vision of a place where thinkers and lovers of literature can evolve a shareable language. At the end of *any* critical revolution, we are left with jargon. Words like "logocentrism" or "differance" are a stink given off by the corpse of that movement known as Deconstructionism. It's important to remember, though, that they once held ideas that were, for a time, useful in finding a new vantage point on literature, in creating a common ground for thinkers about literature.

Before, I spoke of James Wood. His early work is, for me, exemplary of the worst of criticism (or reviewing) as plastic surgery. If one enjoyed the theatre of operations, one could regularly catch Dr. Wood cutting away work that he felt wasn't worthy of the pursuit that is "great literature." But with *How Fiction Works* something important has changed. Though *How Fiction*

Works doesn't acknowledge its own prejudices and assumptions, James Wood has begun to move away from judgement and towards the contemplation of ideas ("free indirect style," "detail," the nature of "character" in fiction, etc.) that might serve as a useful ground from which we can all talk about novels or short stories. Today's preoccupation with free indirect style has the potential to become the next decade's "phallogo-centrism," but it was startling to read Wood write of David Foster Wallace and Thomas Pynchon with an eye not primarily to a dismissal of "hysterical realism" but, rather, to an understanding of the necessity, the *logic* of their creation. And in that *possibility* of under-standing there is what is best about theory: the brief — inevitably brief, because every generation has to renovate the language and idea of criticism — sense that literature is one of the most startling things we humans do, our hive-making, our adaptive coloration.

Asylum

During the eighties and early nineties, times were good for writers. Advances were generous. Survival as a writer was a slightly easier proposition for some of us than it had been in the past.

After I sold my first book *Despair and Other Stories of Ottawa*, I was encouraged to write a novel. (Though people speak with respect of Alice Munro and Mavis Gallant, short stories are still a difficult sell in our country.) So, I wrote a novel: *Childhood*. It did well enough and earned a generous advance on my next adult novel. I then wrote a children's book called *Ingrid and the Wolf*. It also did well. That is, it was nominated for an award.

I then spent ten years writing a book about Ottawa, a novel whose objective was to chronicle the city's complications of morality and language and foreign influence. *Asylum*, the novel in question, was an effort to pack up all that Ottawa has meant to me and arrange it in the confines of a novel, where it would be kept safe.

Asylum hasn't made back its advance. It received mostly good reviews, but the book did not sell, nor was it nominated for any awards. Worse: during the ten years it had taken me to fit Ottawa neatly into *Asylum*, the publishing landscape changed. Publishers, losing money in difficult financial times, are now skittish. *Childhood*'s success made *Asylum* possible, but *Asylum* may make *Pastoral*, my next novel, more difficult — an interesting turn of events for a novelist.

I am writing this sentence on January 5, 2010. I am fifty-two years old, unsure if I can go on writing as I have previously. More likely, things will be different. Perhaps Norman Levine's stories of the writing life — I'm thinking in particular of one in which a writer goes to his school reunion and quietly bums money off each of his former classmates — will once again be relevant.

Was *Asylum* a "failure," then?

Well, for its publishers, I suppose it may be disappointing. And yet, two years later, I think it's still too early to say. *Pro captu lectoris habent sua fata libelli*: books have their fates in the capacities of their readers. So, *Asylum*'s time may come when it meets another set of readers.

And for *Asylum*'s readers? Here, as always, "failure" is as partial as "success." Some will like a work, others will not. It's the fate of any book to meet with acceptance *and* rejection. So, "failure" is difficult to gauge and "success" tends to be measurable mostly in monetary terms.

Finally, did I accomplish the artistic goals I set out to accomplish when I began the book? Yes, I did. The book I finished is very different from the book I set out to write, but the book I wrote is the one I *needed* to write. Characters and situations led me to the (somewhat unexpected) harbour that is the final draft. Would I have written *Asylum* differently, knowing what I know now? No, because I'm not so in control of my psyche that I can force it to do my bidding. And novels are an affair as much of the psyche as of the reasoning part of oneself.

More interesting than all of these questions of supposed "success" or presumed "failure" is the question of how *Asylum* lives within my psyche now. Its failure to please on a wide enough scale has been an invitation to reconsider what writing means to me and what I hope to accomplish as a writer. *Childhood* brought no such soul searching. So, in a curious way, *Childhood*'s "success" does not belong to me as much as *Asylum*'s "failure" does.

As one might expect, the most annoying thing about this constant consideration and reconsideration of a book you've just finished is the self-doubt it brings.[34] Was I meant to be a writer at all, I wonder? Yes, of course. Is there any other career I can take up? No, it's too late. Do I have the courage to carry on with my literary aspirations and visions, whatever the pressure of the marketplace? Yes. In my worst moments, when self-doubt keeps me awake, it helps to recall why I came to Toronto (to write), why I wanted to write (to imagine the range of possibilities hidden in the word "home"), and why writing matters to me (because there are books I love, books I want to write, and because there

---

34 There are strangely amusing aspects to this, as well. One feels as if one could gauge how well or poorly one is doing by how quickly or slowly one is able to talk to one's editor, say, or one's agent. It takes longer to get *anyone* on the phone. And the quality of silence following a work's misfiring is as characteristic as the sound of an altar bell rung in an empty church.

are words, like *tootoolbay* or *kunumunu*, *wajank* or *waheen*, that bring such pleasure.[35] There are moments when, thinking of words or of writing, I can still feel the strength of my commitment to the art form that has chosen me.

Other Books

Whatever the disappointments of "literary society," however distressing it is to imagine that literature is a thing in decline because our thinking about it is shallow, and although the bewilderment at having written an unpopular book is, well, bewildering, there are still works I admire, books that remind me of why I want to keep writing. There are actually quite a number of them. In the last twenty years my contemporaries have written some very fine books (or plays) and I could happily write about any number — from Margaret Visser's *The Geometry of Love* to Darren O'Donnell's *Radio Rooster Says That's Bad*. But I'm not a completist and, besides,

---

35   There are many words I love, but words from Trinidad are especially consoling. *Tootoolbay* means distracted, confused, or bewildered by feelings of love — or just plain attraction — for someone of the opposite sex. It comes from the French *tout troublé*. A kunumunu is an idiot. I heard it used by a man, unhappy with his wife's affection for another man, screaming, "Yuh t'ink I's a fuckin' *kunumunu*?" Then again, his wife was a *wajank*. That is: a loud, obstreperous woman. (Not to be confused with a *waheen*, a woman of loose morals, perhaps even an amateur prostitute.) In a sentence: "But Marlene is a real wajank, yuh heah? How de France yuh could love she?"

the contemplation of a handful of books has brought me solace and pleasure these past few months and I'd like to talk about *them*: *Short Journey Upriver toward Oishida*, *Eunoia*, *Hunger's Brides*, *Muriella Pent*, and *The Woodcutter*. It is, of course, impossible to give a complete or even adequate account of such absorbing and suggestive books in the space of this memoir. Still, I'd like to talk about aspects of them that have caught my attention.

1. Roo Borson's Short Journey Upriver toward Oishida

For my money, *Short Journey Upriver toward Oishida* is the single most impressive collection of poems written in Canada in quite some time. You could point to books of poetry in which individual poems are more immediately accessible than those in *Short Journey*. For instance, in Don McKay's *Night Field*, the poem "Moth Fear" moved me deeply the first time I read it (in K's living room, dim light from a window that looked onto the brick wall of the house next door) and has stayed with me since. None of the poems in *Short Journey* got to me so quickly. But I have lived with *Short Journey* for some time now, having read it closely and been drawn repeatedly back to it, and the book has so grown in my imagination that I can't think of any recent book of Canadian poetry I would take in its place.

The most obvious thing about *Short Journey* is that it is a kind of anti *ars poetica*. Rather than declaring what poetry is and how it should be done, Roo begins, in the poem "Summer Grass," with a question: "Do you still love poetry?" It isn't a rhetorical question. All of the pieces that follow struggle, either in their structure or in their sound, to capture some inkling or quality of what poetry is, so that the question can be given a meaningful answer. Not a definitive answer. There is no definitive answer to the question "What is poetry?" As a consequence, there can be no definitive answer to Roo's "Do you still love poetry?" either. The journey, in *Short Journey Upriver toward Oishida*, is towards poetry itself, *upriver* towards a possible source, but the source is not attained. The final lines of the book are

Early in the morning or else past sundown,
at evening, dusk,
the wind through the open window,
the radio on and the unopened map beside
    you —

A strophe, incomplete, ending with a dash, suggesting imminent departure, not arrival.

One of the aspects of the book that seems to have puzzled reviewers is its use of prose. If you accept that a definition or understanding of *poetry* is at the heart of

Roo's search, however, the use of prose makes simple, lucid sense. Poetry is usually defined in relation to prose. In simplistic terms, poetry is what prose is not and vice versa. By juxtaposing moments of poetry with moments of prose, *Short Journey* pushes the poetic element of poetry into the foreground, doesn't it? Well, yes and no. *Short Journey* is a book that refuses simple answers. Yes, the section called "A Bit of History" — which is *about* poetry — is prose-like compared to the more traditional poems in the section "Water Colour." But "Autumn Record" (the most beautiful part of the book, I think) is filled with prose poems, and the long, narrative prose piece "Persimmons" is suffused with poetry: in its quality of observation, in its elegiac tone, in its juxtaposition of intimacy and death:

> These nights, to get to sleep, I imagine a
> bullet entering the back of my head.

In other words, *Short Journey* also raises the question of what, exactly, "prose" is.

Another reason for the "prose" in *Short Journey* is a little less obvious: *Short Journey Upriver toward Oishida* is influenced by the seventeenth-century Japanese poet Matsuo Basho. No, that's to put it too casually. *Short Journey* is written with Basho in mind, with Basho's poetry as both guidance and accompanying music. *Short Journey* is a work of devotion to and an argument with the work of Basho. And throughout *Short Journey*, the choice of Basho as "master" is deeply felt and has great influence on the texts. What that has to do with Roo's "prose" is this: Basho's *Oku no Hosomichi*, or *Narrow Road to the Deep North*, is a travel narrative in which prose and poetry intermingle. In fact, the majority of *Narrow Road* is what we would call "prose," but some of that "prose" is clearly poetic. *Narrow Road* is one of those works that suggest, without ever saying so, that the poetic is something other than words disposed on a page according to certain rules (Basho's haiku, for instance).

Poetry, for Basho, is the thing that may be captured by words but that is not confined to them. As Basho has it, there is an "everlasting self that is poetry." That "self" is both the poet and not the poet. It's possible to speak of Basho's "self" as being the land, for instance, so that the commentator who said of *Narrow Road* that "it is as if the very soul of Japan had itself written it" was getting at something crucial to Basho's idea of poetry: neither the land nor the man speaks, but "poetry" is.

This sense of the land — an affection and respect for it — comes through in *Short Journey*. The various landscapes of California, Japan, Australia, China, and Canada are scrutinized by the poet. But there's something more to all this. Roo's *Short Journey* is not simply about "poetry." It is also about death and aging and the impermanent. Here even the natural world is compared to music, that most fleeting of things. But poetry as Basho understood it is, at least potentially, a *lasting* thing. And in *Short Journey*, there is the suggestion — or is it the hope? — that poetry can contain and keep the fleeting and the gone. In *Short Journey* the "fleeting and the gone" includes childhood summers in California, time spent in Australia, boys and girls who have gone from one's life, and, above all, one's parents. The deaths of Roo's parents is a wound, and part of the pain this wound inflicts is the anxiety that those one loves will fade. So, in *Short Journey*, Roo's search for "poetry" is also a search for some "thing" which will keep safe that which she fears might vanish forever.

There is much, much more to say about *Short Journey*, about its language in particular, which is subtly, and at times humourously, playful,[36] and about the

---

36 Actually, yes, a few words about Roo's language . . . It's easy, with a poet like Roo, to miss the playfulness of her work. The seriousness of her purpose, the fact she is associated with "ecopoets" like Tim Lilburn or Jan Zwicky, and the chasteness of her language blinds people to lines like

            . . . For ague:
    read the old books in which ague is still argued
or
    Everything is manufactured by Mattel. If there were a hell
    it would be spring, the tortures of the chrysalis . . .
or

book's first section, "Summer Grass," a sometimes difficult but necessary preface of sorts, in which Roo catalogues what is lost. But I want to end this brief consideration of the book by mentioning one aspect of *Short Journey* that hasn't yet elicited much commentary: the oscillating, equal-space-occupying existence of seventeenth-century Japan and twenty-first-century North America in the book.

It isn't just that Roo exists and, simultaneously, Basho exists as well, in her use of his words, his imagery, his concision, and his profound respect for nature, which she shares. It's something more. When asked, "What makes a poet's language distinctive?" Margaret Avison answered, "It is saying 'I am here and not not-there.'" This is a good way not only of suggesting what makes poetic language "distinctive" but, beyond

---

                                        . . . And tonight
          the half-light in which paper glows —
          walls, porticos, arches, palaces (who lived there?),
          the print invisible, and the ocean sounding
          all night long, clavicle to vena cava,
          clavicle to vena cava . . .

In *Short Journey Upriver toward Oishida*, Roo employs internal rhyme, repetition, consonance (". . . *the world the whorls of weather* . . ."), assonance, all manner of sound play that is suddenly there and then as quickly gone. It's all the more striking because the wordplay bubbles out of a poetic language that is deliberately restrained so that it can accommodate, with little conflict, the poetry of Meng Haoran, Matsuo Basho, and Jane Munro, as well as the strong echoes of those who have influenced her, T. S. Eliot in particular.

that, of nailing one of the characteristics of poetry in general and of *Short Journey* in particular. "Here and not not-there" is descriptive of the relationship of Roo Borson to her mentor Matsuo Basho, but it also captures the *feeling* of Roo's poetry in *Short Journey*, a book that is thrilling in its erotics of the relational.

2. *Christian Bök's* Eunoia

Just before *Eunoia* was published, Christian spoke to me about the process of writing the book. We were at a Russell Smith book launch, I think, and Christian described the writing of *Eunoia* as "disturbing," in that it filled him with a kind of paranoia, the feeling that language was using him for its own purposes. Not in the usual way ("My characters took over from me and wrote the book themselves"), but in a way more sinister. While writing a passage containing only such words as use the vowel *e*

> Whenever Helen sleeps, her essence enters the ether —
> the deep well, where she feels herself descend deeper,
> deeper.

it was, he said, as if he could feel the "mind" of language compelling him to say the things he said, whether he wanted to say them or not. In the case of *Eunoia's* Chapter E, it felt as if he'd had no choice but to cough up a version of *The Iliad*, the last thing he'd set out to do.

Having just written of Basho's "everlasting self," it seems appropriate to ask what, exactly, was guiding Christian's work.

Eunoia is a puzzling book whose most intriguing puzzles are hidden behind a formal apparatus that, though impressive in its execution, is actually kind of monotonous. The book is a short noem (novel/poem) or, if you like, a long povel (poem/novel) whose five chapters are exercises in univocalism.[37] Along with the univocalisms, *Eunoia* was written with certain other constraints. Among these: all the chapters had to allude to the art of writing; all had to include a scene of banqueting, of sexual debauchery, of nautical voyaging; and each chapter had to describe a pastoral vista. As I said: intriguing, but kind of monotonous. Christian's real innovation is that, in *Eunoia*, each of the vowels is given its own chapter (Chapter A, Chapter E, Chapter I, Chapter O, Chapter U), and this allows the reader to *hear* the character of *a*, the character of *e*, and so on. For the reader, as well as for the author, it's as if one can sense a personality in each of the vowels, a personality that changes from chapter to chapter (vowel to vowel) and grows stronger by the

---

37   In the *Oulipo Compendium*, a univocalist text is described as "one written with a single vowel." And the *Compendium*'s editors, Harry Mathews and Alistair Brotchie, imagine the beginning of Hamlet's monologue as written by a univocalistically inclined Shakespeare: *"Be? Never be? Perplexed quest: seek the secret!"*

juxtapositions the chapters create. Here's a sentence from each chapter:

> Awkward grammar appals a craftsman.
> Enfettered, these sentences repress free speech.
> Sighing, I sit, scribbling in ink this pidgin script.
> Loops on bold fonts now form lots of words for books.
> Bulls plus bucks run thru buckbrush; thus dun burrs
> clutch fur tufts.[38]

On another occasion entirely—this time, at Harbourfront, I think—Christian spoke of his distaste for "personal detail" in poetry. Confessional poetry, he said, left him unimpressed, because it usually generated easy emotion or appealed to (and sometimes won) the reader's emotional involvement by going around the aesthetic. Meaning: confessional poetry could generate emotional responses whether or not it was good poetry. It relied on biographical data, on things *outside* the art of poetry for its effect. A cheat, he thought. His own poetry was resolutely *im*personal. If anything, his work is—like Basho's, though very, very few people would think of Basho while reading *Crystallography* or *Eunoia*—attuned to some essential aspect of poetry. (An "essence" that is not

---

38 I would have included a sentence on the art of writing from Chapter U, as I did from the other chapters, but *Eunoia*'s only "failure" is in Chapter U's non-inclusion of any conspicuous allusion to the art of writing.

necessarily the preserve of humans. One of Christian's favourite books, at the time of *Eunoia*, was a collection of poems generated by a computer program.[39])

These two things — the fact that Christian found writing *Eunoia* a paranoia-inducing experience and the fact that he avoids the biographical in his own work — are interesting when taken together. They suggest that Christian both courts the "purely poetic" (or pure language) and is frightened by it. But I have another question about *Eunoia*, a political one, that sharpens the question about Christian's role in creating *Eunoia*. Here's an excerpt from Chapter O:

> Porno shows folks lots of sordor — zoom
> shots of Bjorn Borg's bottom or Snoop

---

39 Here is a poem generated by Raymond Kurzweil's Cybernetic Poet, a program designed to write poetic texts based on models it has been fed. That is, the programmer feeds poetry into the program then asks the program to create poetry of its own, and the *Cybernetic Poet* creates poems. In this case, an imperfect haiku:

Soul
You broke my soul
the juice of eternity,
the spirit of my lips.

Or, in this next case, a rather more Robert Creeley–influenced meditation:

Wondered
today i wondered
if i mused
today i saw you

Dogg's crotch. Johns who don condoms for
blowjobs go downtown to Soho to look for
pornshops known to stock lots of lowbrow
shlock — off-colour porn for old boors who
long to drool onto color photos of cocks,
boobs, dorks or dongs. Homos shoot photos
of footlong shlongs.

Now, Christian is North American. He knows that,
in North America at least, black men are commonly
reduced to being "mere penises" as a way of suggesting they aren't fully, intellectually equal to white men.
So, why does he (or why does the text) point to Snoop
Dogg's crotch, reducing Snoop Dogg to his dick? Further, he knows that "homo" is an insulting epithet for

---

i learned
in awe and you
if i wondered
if i mused
today i had one wish
if i saw you
if i saw you
if i had one wish

One of the amusing paradoxes of Christian's love for computer-generated
poetry is that, though the Cybernetic Poet program, for instance, has no
"life" as we understand the word, it still produces work that has "biographical" details, confessional moments that, from a *human* poet, Christian would find unconvincing and unimpressive. And yet, you couldn't
exactly accuse Christian of being inconsistent. Any "confessional" aspect I
see in the program's poetry is an aspect added by me, isn't it?

"homosexual." If you accept that this passage is racist or homophobic, to whom does the racism or homophobia belong? To Christian? Or to language itself?

I want to be absolutely clear, before we go on: I would bet my life on the fact that Christian Bök is *not* racist, nor have I ever known him to be homophobic. Moreover, I think the passage about "Snoop Dogg" and "homos" could be qualified as (at worst) *insensitive* rather than "racist" or "homophobic." But what I'm pointing to here is a tension that runs through *Eunoia* like an electric current: Christian-language, language-Christian, like "zero" and "one" in computer programming. Let's think it through a little: the *only* reason Snoop Dogg is in *Eunoia* is that his name is univocalic. "Snoop Dogg" has been reduced to letters on a page. "Bjorn Borg" is here for the same reason. Neither man is referred to in relation to his real self. They're simply words on a page. So, from one angle, any racism at play here is the by-product of certain rules that generated the text. Or, more emphatically put: the racism is in the reader, not the text, nor the rules that generated it, because rules can't be racist any more than computer programs can feel longing. But how would the reader feel about the passage I quoted if the text had read (in part)

> Porno shows folks lots of sordor — zoom shots of Bjorn Borg's crotch or Snoop Dogg's bottom.

In this form, you lose the alliteration of "Bjorn Borg's bottom" (a lovely sound, although, as to the phenomenon itself . . . having spent some time searching for pictures of Bjorn Borg's bottom online, I'd have to say it is not one of the man's commonly featured features) but you also lose the allusion to Snoop Dogg's crotch and, so, lessen (perhaps!) the possibility of a race-conscious reading. Well? Is it, politically, *more* acceptable to talk about "Snoop Dogg's" butt?

Actually, my question is more specific. I mean to ask: is it more acceptable, politically, for Christian (a white man) to write about a black man's crotch or the same black man's arse? To accept that the passage *could* be other than as Christian wrote it is what I'm getting at. To admit that Christian has made important choices unconnected to the rules that generated *Eunoia* is to begin to question the necessity of *Eunoia* as we have it. It is to see *Eunoia* as a long series of micro-choices that, cumulatively, tell us things about *Christian*, not about the rules used to generate the text or about the "mind" of poetry/language. In this sense, *Eunoia* is a very peculiar autobiography.

Perhaps the most revealing moments in the book are in the afterwords, a section called "The New Ennui," in which Christian talks about the procedures he used to generate *Eunoia*. He writes, among other things,

... *Eunoia* is directly inspired by the exploits of Oulipo (l'Ouvroir de Littérature Poten-tielle) — the avant-garde coterie renowned for its literary experimentation with extreme formalistic constraints. The text makes a Sisy-phean spectacle of its labour, wilfully crip-pling its language in order to show that, even under such improbable conditions of duress, language can still express an uncanny, if not sublime, thought.

Two curious things in this passage. First, the Oulipo began as a group of writers and mathematicians who sought not to bind and constrain literary creation, but, inspired by Bourbaki (the name of a collective of mathematicians), to find ways to combine the arts of literature and mathematics. Constraints are *one* aspect of *some* of the Oulipo's procedures. Obliga-tions (things that must be done within a text . . . the Baron in Calvino's *Baron in the Trees*, for instance, must remain up in his trees all his life) and alterations (creation using previously existing texts) are among the others. Christian chooses to mention only one aspect of the Oulipo's work, and he refers to it in a tell-ing way: "extreme formalistic constraints." I think it's safe to say that not only does he see things this way but also that this is what he *needs* from the Oulipo. Even more interesting, Christian speaks of the *text* making a spectacle of its labour, of the *text* wilfully crippling its language, so that *language* can express an uncanny (unsettling, as if of supernatural origin or nature) or sublime thought. In Christian's own terminology a violence has been done, but language did it to itself, with him as its — what? — servant? handmaid?

With *Eunoia*, we enter into a kind of dark region in which the relationship between the writer and language is a form of sadomasochism out of which "poetry" comes.

The text of *Eunoia* is, at times, incredibly beautiful and amusing. It's unlike any other written in my country. Chapter E, its retelling of the myth of Helen, is stunning. And one could, as some critics have, write for days about its wordplay.

To me, though, *Eunoia* is surprisingly similar to *Short Journey Upriver toward Oishida*: both texts are overt questionings of the idea of "poetry," the writers of both have foreign mentors (Basho, the Oulipo), and both works give the reader an inkling of the relational (Avison's "here and not not-there": Basho/Roo, Constraints/Christian). *Eunoia* is a compellingly disturbed field, where *Short Journey* is very still. Both works hide, on first reading, as much as they show. *Short Journey* hides by staying quiet. *Eunoia* hides by making a loud spectacle of itself.

Two versions of doubt. Fascinating books, both of them.

3. *Paul Anderson's* Hunger's Brides

Hunger's Brides is a mystery novel, an eccentric one, with two central mysteries. The first concerns the disappearance of a brilliant graduate student named Beulah Limosneros. For this part of the novel, her lover and thesis adviser, Donald Gregory, is our "detective." The second mystery concerns the seventeenth-century Mexican poet Sor Juana Inés de la Cruz, who, when she was at the height of her creative power, abandoned — or was forced to abandon — the writing of poetry. Our "detective," here, is Beulah Limosneros, whose biography of Sor Juana makes up a good portion of the novel's 1,300 pages.

Early in the first chapter, Donald Gregory warns us about the book we're reading. He warns us by telling us about himself. He writes, "If you want to better understand the true, study the liar." He then offers an expansion of the idea: one of the ways we might arrive at knowledge of God is by knowing all the things God is *not*. This is the *via negativa*, the "negative road" to knowledge, and Gregory tells us that he made his reputation in academia by writing essays whose thesis was that fiction is a *via negativa*, a lie that leads to the truth or, as pertinently, the sacred. In other words, for the novel's narrator, the novel we're reading is less important for what it says than for what it leaves *unsaid*, or for what it implies.

This is the novel's first explicit statement of a dichotomy (truth/lie) as well as the introduction of a dynamic that courses through the novel. *Hunger's Brides* is filled with couples and doubles: Donald/Beulah, Beulah/Sor Juana Inés de la Cruz, Juana/Amanda, Canada/Mexico, past/present, self/other, poetry/prose, postmodern/baroque.[40] With so many couples and doubles, it's almost natural that the novel is riven by an anxiety about the "true": the true poetic image, the true translation, the true story of Sor Juana Inés de la Cruz, the true story of Beulah's disappearance. There is even some question about the true book since, by the end, it's difficult to say just who the narrator of the book we've read actually is: Beulah Limosneros or her professor/lover Donald Gregory.

If, in Margaret Avison's terms, poetry is relational and writes from its relationality ("here and not not-there"), *Hunger's Brides* is an instance in which prose lives out its anxiety about "here or there-ness." And a part of that anxiety is about the tools we use to see the

---

40   In one of Beulah's notebooks, I think it is, the ornate and sometimes obscure imagery and narrative strategies of Baroque art are mirrored by the postmodern art of our time. This is another of the book's warnings that, here, we are on a Rococo road.

world. For instance, *Hunger's Brides* is a novel of mirrors that is wary of mirrors.[41]

Of course, this is not a work by Kafka or Poe. It uses its anxiety more playfully. It makes "truth" its object while parodying various genres that have "the true" as their objective: mystery stories, detective fiction, translations, literary criticism, historical research, theological disputes. It also runs the gamut of modes of expression—poetry, non-fiction, fiction, movie scripts—as if testing the ways of writing in order to find the *right* one for its purposes or, in keeping with Professor Gregory's thinking, to exhaust the *human* ways of speaking in order to leave the divine. An interesting objective and one that *requires* the 1,300 pages the novel uses, if not more.

The novel is complex, ambitious, playful, strange, and instructive. There are any number of ways to talk about it, any number of facets to be considered. But the aspect of the novel that moved me most is its embrace of hybridity. The novel is a document of the cultural moment we live in. It's a thing built out of the multiple origins of my country, of our country. The way its parts

---

41   *Literally* wary of mirrors. In a striking passage, we learn that the god Tezcatlipoca — "one of the most haunting visions of divinity ever conjured by the collective imagination" — is known as "Broken Face, He-who-causes-things-to-be-seen-in-a-mirror." The narrator then switches registers and tells us that "for the philosophy of knowledge, a mirror's distortions were a troublesome source of altered perceptions — calling into question, in the age of Descartes, every man's faith in the data of his senses."

interact — influencing and counter-influencing each other — give an inkling of Canada's (and Mexico's) culturally hybrid nature. This is especially the case as concerns the *language* of Juana de la Cruz.

Reviewing the novel in *The Independent*, Tim Martin asserts that

> You can tell the protagonists are Spanish because they talk in Spanish: "This single book is why, en mi opinión, the many generations of us who followed Cortes have not raised a monument to him." Anderson is keen for his readers not to miss any of his tricks, even if that does mean diluting the effect to explain things to smaller intellects than his own.

This is shoddy and self-satisfied reviewing. The point is not that the protagonists "talk in Spanish." They manifestly do not. This is a novel in *English*. The speech of the Mexican characters includes Spanish phrases. It is mixed, a hybrid. Nor is this done so that Paul Anderson can "explain things to smaller intellects than his own," though, on the evidence, Tim Martin's intellect needs all the help it can get. If he had bothered to read the footnotes, the reviewer might have read a pertinent passage on accent, translation, and "authenticity." The choice to include Spanish phrases in the dialogue of the

242

Spanish speakers was made precisely to indicate that the Spanish speakers had been translated (or, better, transplanted) into this English narrative. The Spanish words and phrases are used to heighten the *foreignness* of the Spanish language in the text, as well as to point to the crazed translator/interpreter of Sor Juana's thoughts, poetry, and intellectual life: Beulah Limosneros.[42]

Something else about the language of Sor Juana Inés de la Cruz: from the start, it's clear we are dealing with a particular version of Sor Juana. The young Sor Juana reads Herodotus and Thucydides, Plato and Aristotle. She reads all the books found in her grandfather's library, and is traumatized about such things as the fifth-century massacre of the inhabitants of Melos by the Athenian forces. That is to say, Beulah

---

42 I guess this is as good a place as any to have a digression on footnotes. The footnotes in *Hunger's Brides* are strange. One is not always certain if the books they refer to are real, if the annotator is Donald Gregory or Beulah Limosneros or even Paul Anderson. They are part of the novel's fictional warp and weave. Some are instructive, others maddening and arch. But all of them are suggestive of the different strata at play in the novel.

To speak of more personal matters, however . . . footnotes have always brought me solace. It is as if one can both say something and, in an instant, have it unsaid. A friend recently said of me, "Ask him the same question five minutes after he's answered it, and you'll get a different answer." This is, to a great extent, true. Nothing in my world seems to stand up for long. A footnote is a means of escape. And it is one of the disappointments of my writing life that publishers (word processors too, for that matter) don't allow footnotes in footnotes. Or footnotes in footnotes in footnotes. The idea of an infinite regress, an abyss of footnotes, brings me not angst but peace of mind. The line that separates thought from counter-thought or thought from supplementary thought is like a placid surface of a body of water.

243

Limosneros's Sor Juana speaks as if she were much older. This is a somewhat conventional approach. After all, intelligence doesn't always reveal itself quite so directly outside the realm of fiction. But then there is the poetry. In *Hunger's Brides*, Sor Juana's poetry is a kind of absolute, as close to the divine as the novel *directly* gets. Her poetry is given, at times, in Spanish:

> Este, que ves, engaño colorido
> que del arte ostentando los primores,
> con falso silogismos de colores
> es cauteloso engaño del sentido;

or in the translations of Beulah Limosneros

> This painted semblance you so admire,
> of an art flaunting its mastery
> with false syllogisms of colour,
> that smoothly mocks the eye;

or translated by "real" translators.[43] Her poems are sifted to give up their secrets. But Sor Juana's poetry is also a kind of bedrock from which the novel springs.

---

43 If the novel has a significant flaw it is, I think, that Beulah Limosneros's translations are not up to Sor Juana's work. (Beulah's sometimes overwrought imagery — throughout the novel — is also a bit of a problem.

In this, *Hunger's Brides* calls to mind (to my mind, at least) Vladimir Nabokov's translation of *Eugene Onegin*. Yes, Nabokov's *Onegin* is a different kind of beast: a literal translation of Pushkin's long poem. But in his copious volumes of footnotes, Nabokov tries to restore to the Russian words their context, their sonic and psychological implications, their playfulness. Nabokov's real accomplishment and originality was in trying to translate (to bring into the English language) what lay *behind* Pushkin's Russian words, to have in the foreground things that usually get lost altogether in translation.

So it is, too, with *Hunger's Brides*. In bringing the Baroque to life in the text, in restoring some of the historical drama of Sor Juana's time, in devising a reading of Sor Juana's work that is grounded in the poetry as well as in the *foreignness* of the poetry, Anderson has gone some way to pointing to the things in

The novel is, at times, extremely *writerly*.) But Beulah's translations raise interesting questions. Paul Anderson, in creating Beulah's translations, has created a particular translator. I mean: the *style* of Beulah's translations is revealing of Beulah's character. So, in novelistic terms, Beulah's translations are, in fact, perfect revelations of her personality — perfect translations for the novel — while still "betraying" Sor Juana's work. Actually, an interesting essay could be written about what her translations tell us about Beulah, the fictional character. Beulah is less retrained, less poised, less "Aristotelian" than Sor Juana. The poem I've quoted, one of Sor Juana's most memorable, is one in which she speaks of the ways art can deceive. An alternative translation to Beulah's, one more faithful to Sor Juana, might read orbit around the poetry itself, worlds usually lost in translation: words, of course, words and sounds and ideas that have directly influenced the world. *Hunger's Brides* seems to me to be about the worlds that Sor Juana's work has called into being, about poetry's deep, subterranean influence or, to echo Shelley: it's about the kind of legislation poets (unacknowledged) carry out.

4. *Russell Smith's* Muriella Pent

For me, *Muriella Pent* is the best novel of Toronto written by a contemporary of mine. It is flawed, certainly. It is sometimes flat in its social satire — for instance, in its repeated skewering of "political correctness" (which is, at the end of the day, a rather large, unmoving target). But if I were asked to name the novel that best captured something essential about the Toronto I've known, I could think of no serious competition.

> This, that you see, this coloured treachery,
> which, by displaying all the charms of art,
> with those false syllogisms of its hues
> deceptively subverts the sense of sight;
> (translated by Alix Ingber, 1995)

or

> These lying pigments facing you,
> with every charm brush can supply
> set up false premises of color
> to lead astray the human eye.
> (translated by Alan Trueblood, 1988)

246

The book is squirm-inducing, partisan, amusing, complex, and original. I almost understand why it won no major book award.[44] *Muriella Pent* is such an acid portrait of Toronto it's difficult to know just how to deal with the book or where to put it. It doesn't fit beside *Cat's Eye* or *In the Skin of a Lion*, still less beside *Fugitive Pieces* or the university-centred fantasies of Robertson Davies. It's a work clearly influenced by Amis *père* and Evelyn Waugh, but also by unexpected countercurrents. *Muriella Pent* is satirical, sure, but beneath the satire there's a surrealist mechanism at work, one that is, perhaps, missed by reviewers who tend to focus on the targets of the work's satire and on how well (or poorly) the novel hits them.

Of course, the novel invites such a focus because its surface is so provocative: a Caribbean poet named

---

44 I do find the critical reception of Russell's work a little odd, though. He is among our best writers of prose. (He switches registers — jumping from, say, nerd speak to university pukka — at will and convincingly.) His work is resolutely fixed on the present and so offers an interesting portrait of Toronto and its inhabitants. Just what people want, you'd think. But, aside from the Governor General's Literary Award nomination for *How Insensitive*, there's little sign that his novels are taken as seriously as those of, say, Joseph Boyden, who, as a writer of prose, is at times inept. (By which I mean: Boyden's worst sentences telegraph their meaning or use adverbs to "heighten" moments that are already emotionally charged. It's inefficient writing.) I was reminded of Russell's "occlusion" by an article in the *National Post* written by Barbara Kay. Kay had, without reading it, trashed a novel by Lisa Moore. An indefensibly stupid thing to do, but, as I mentioned above, the *Post* is not a particularly relevant forum for literary discussion. Kay then wrote a second article in which she stated,

Marcus Royston is invited to be part of a cultural exchange program in Toronto. Though he is a writer of some reputation, he is chosen less for his talent than for the fact he is from a "third world" country: the island of St Andrew's. The selection committee, dominated by its politically sensitive but self-righteous members, hopes that his presence in Toronto will teach Toronto's arts communities about "real" suffering. Royston is put up in the home of a wealthy, white bluestocking named Muriella Pent, a woman for whom the committee members feel disdain because of her wealth and social standing. Confusion, both sexual and political, ensues and comes to a head at a party thrown *chez* Mrs. Pent.

The meetings of the "Arts Action Committee," the group charged with choosing the writer who will come to Toronto, are particularly well done. The depictions

---

Several readers admonished me for unfairly pre-judging the novel. Coincidentally Moore's editor sent me not only the Moore novel, but the publishing house of Anansi's entire CanLit list of 2009 authors. Duly chastened, I packed them all up for my vacation. Five of the novels I was sent and that I read some of — by authors Gil Adamson, Rawi Hage (two), Bill Gaston, and Peter Behrens — are beautifully written, and seem to have vivid plots, but take place elsewhere (Ireland, Lebanon) and/or in the distant past. That's one CanLit premise: Nothing happening in our present history outside the self — say, oh, I dunno, how about the real-life story of a brilliant, creative, Canada-changing newspaper baron brought low by circumstances and a tragically flawed character — seems worthy of fictional treatment to Canadian novelists.

are cruel and funny. In the first of the committee meetings we attend, the intestinal distress of eating too many chickpeas is nicely rendered. It begins like this:

> "I want to propose," said Deepak, "that we end the blind business."
>
> There was a silence filled with sticky chewing. Brian got up to get some more food. He hesitated between the chickpea roti and the chickpea salad.
>
> Jasminka, at the head of the table, and Iris Warshavsky seemed to be struggling with their rotis. The ends of the wrapped bread had grown ragged and were leaking chickpeas in gravy. The conference table was speckled with errant chickpeas. Mrs.

Now, this is the kind of dishonesty that makes Kay difficult to take seriously. In her trashing of Lisa Moore, Kay complained that "CanLit" novels were short on dialogue, action, and plot. Here, finding novels that *do* have vivid plots, she criticizes them for being set elsewhere (you could criticize Hemingway or Henry James for the same thing: setting novels in Europe) or in the past (*War and Peace* is due some stick, on the same grounds). In effect, Kay defines "CanLit" as being only what she says it is (plotless, storyless, filled with sensitive women and feminized men, set in the past or in another country) and then thrashes it, administering a sound beating to her own straw man. "CanLit" (a designation that shouldn't be used without proper definition) is more — and different (why should it not include Guy Gavriel Kay, for instance?) — than that which is crucified by Barbara Kay. The reason I mention her article at all is that Russell Smith has been, for some time, writing novels with plots, with "unfeminized"

Pent was using her plastic fork to pick at a salad on the plate before her. She said, "Do we do things with the blind?"

All of the novel's characters are articulate, expressive, self-absorbed, and, most of them, well intentioned. Marcus Royston, the "third world" poet, is melancholy, somewhat depraved, disillusioned, sarcastic, and emotionally complex. Muriella is not as complicated. She is a widow recently freed from her husband's stifling presence, and she is beginning to explore her creative side. She is sympathetically drawn, however, and her struggle to get out of the straitjacket in which her husband (and her children) have confined her is, at times, moving.

The existential crises of both Marcus and Muriella are nicely dovetailed, played against each other. At the beginning of the novel, we jump from the island of St. Andrew's to the island of "Stilwoode Park," a private enclave in the heart of Toronto, so that, in narrative terms, Marcus and Muriella are a couple — not

---

men, set in the here and now. His work is not "interior"- or "self"-focused. It is, rather, resolutely outward looking, and not particularly leftist. Granted, he hasn't got around to writing about Lord Black of Crossharbour (and, Christ on a fucking cross, I hope it's *Russell* who has to write that novel, not me), but his novels, especially *Muriella Pent*, are such a counter to Kay's notion of "CanLit," it struck me, on reading her article, that I was in the presence of a solid, easily refuted cliché. Valuable to have the cliché, because instructive to recognize it as such.

for nothing do the names begin with M — even before they consummate their relationship.

But before I get to the "surrealist" element in the novel . . . Marcus Royston is a black man depicted, from the first, as sexually rapacious. We meet him through his poetry,[45] through a poem ("Island Eclogues XII") in which his desire to possess a girl is spoken of along with mention of the rapes perpetrated by Jupiter or Apollo. Moreover, when we first meet the man, he is at a bar contemplating the seduction of a Canadian woman who may be useful to him. In effect, then, Russell is, or could be accused of, reducing the black poet to his sexuality. Politically, however, this is a very tricky book. As with Walcott, the use of Greco-Roman myths immediately shows Marcus Royston to be hybrid, one with a foot in at least two worlds. More: the woman he contemplates seducing may be useful to his island, to St. Andrew's, as well as to himself. So, there is an element here of his sexual self being put at the service of others. His sexuality isn't used to *limit* his character or degrade him. It is part of what makes him complex.

Besides, it's the sex in the novel that points to the

---

45 Marcus Royston's poetry is a pastiche of Derek Walcott's work, and it's pretty unconvincing. One has to accept that it is, in the world of *Muriella Pent*, meant to be good poetry. It is, however, the weakest element in the novel. This may be because, being an echo of another's writing, Royston's poetry is the one place where Russell is not himself, a place where he gives precedence to an *idea* rather than to his own ear.

element that runs like an unexpected stratum through it. Now, in some reviews, the sex in *Muriella Pent* was described as a kind of decadence, as if it were an *outré* part of Russell's social critique. It isn't, though, or at least I don't think so. The first hint that something strange is up is in the opening poem in which Marcus compares his sexual desire to the desire of Jupiter or Apollo. Royston aspires to the highest being through the carnal. This is the first linking of Russell's sensibility to the alchemical. In fact, the symbolism in the book is, sometimes conspicuously, alchemical. Aside from Royston's aspiration to a higher being (and *all* the characters aspire to higher states as, in alchemy, all baser metals aspire to the state of gold), the book constantly mentions the sun (or sunlight) and in one passage (in which the narrator describes SkyDome as a bowl or alembic) explicitly speaks of light as gold:

> The roof was peeling back and uncovering a sky vaster, it seemed, than it had been when they were outside. Humid air filled the stadium. There were still clouds blowing quickly across the opened bowl, and the sky between them was a dark blue. One half of the stadium, their half, was flooded with dewy golden light. There was a great majesty to the place, the sheer hugeness of it.

There are other moments of pure alchemy, and one could have a field day with this kind of speculation, pointing out the occurrences of fire, dross, and alembics in the novel. But my purpose isn't to prove anything — it may be that Russell himself is entirely unaware of these correspondences — so much as it is to point out that *Muriella Pent's* story, when looked at from an alchemical angle, is strikingly coherent. A man (Marcus Royston) is introduced to a community of aspirants to culture. He stays in Stilwoode Park — another of the novel's bowls/alembics — where, in the end, he combines (sexually) with a number of people, including Muriella, and the result is that those he has touched (no pun intended) are more aware, better (or "higher") despite their baser elements. As is also appropriate, Marcus Royston, who is the novel's philosopher's stone, is relatively untouched at novel's end. He writes a poem — "In a Cold Climate, Fire" — that is not very different from the poems he has written in the past.

Muriella Pent is at once a social critique (in the tradition of Waugh or Amis) and a version of a pure, alchemical experiment. The book's originality is in the sheer coherence of its own hybridity: a surrealist use of alchemical symbolism existing side by side with Anglo-satire. Russell's two influences easily coexist.

There is much, much more to talk about when it

comes to *Muriella Pent* — for instance, its strikingly beautiful depictions of Toronto or its humour. The book will have, I'd guess, a life after us. But whether that's true or not, it's still the only novel written by a contemporary of mine — or near contemporary, for that matter — which I truly wish I'd written, in part because I share so much of the culture — Caribbean and French, in particular — at the root of the work, and in part because I envy the subtlety with which that culture is put at the service of a narrative vision.

5. *Don Hannah's* The Woodcutter

I wish there were more attention given to play scripts. I understand that a "theatrical event" is much more than the words of the playwright. But "theatre" gets reviewed. Reviewers talk about the actors, the set, the lighting, the direction, while plays themselves, the playwright's words, are very seldom considered on their own merit unless, of course, the play is written by Shakespeare or Beckett or whoever happens to be lustrously dead. This is a common complaint for play-wrights, of course, but there's some justice to it. In Martin Amis's autobiography, *Experience*, Amis sheds the snide opinion that it is ironic that Shakespeare, a playwright, should be the greatest writer of English, when, as we all know, very few playwrights have ever mattered. Amis then challenges the reader of his book to name *any* playwright whose work has lasted beyond a hundred years. Amis's assumption is that few of his readers will be able to name many playwrights after Shakespeare. And, though I hate to admit it, I think he's almost irrefutably right. The average reader is unlikely to know ten great — or even indifferent — playwrights, especially if you take Shakespeare away from them.[46] A sad state of affairs.

---

46   My own ten who've lasted beyond a century — off the top of my head: Aeschylus, Euripides, Aristophanes, Molière, Racine, Corneille, Goethe, Schiller, Georg Büchner, Carlo Goldoni. Then there are the most recent playwrights who will make a century without difficulty: Shaw, Pirandello, Chekhov, Brecht, Beckett, Tennessee Williams, Arthur Miller, Ibsen, Strindberg, Wedekind. Of course, the reason I can name them and make a case for their greatness is that I read plays constantly. My first job in Toronto was as a clerk at Theatrebooks. It's where I picked up my play-reading habit. But as reading plays is something most people *don't* do, perhaps feeling — with some justice — that the "true" play exists principally on a stage, it's hardly surprising the average reader can't name many playwrights.

Playwrighting and poetry: twins. Neither discipline has, in book form, great public support. (If you asked Amis's readers to name ten *poets* who've lasted as long as Shakespeare, you're likely to run into the same inability. I was stunned, while watching a recent BBC documentary on John Donne, to discover that people in the streets of London, asked if they knew who John Donne had been, could not identify the man who is, I think, our language's greatest poet.) Both are forms that require concision and consistent control of voice. I don't suppose it's a coincidence that a number of the playwrights I've mentioned began as poets (Beckett) or wrote poetry at the highest level (Goethe). And then there are playwrights like Heiner Müller or Robert Wilson whose scripts are indistinguishable from poetry: no stage directions, words disposed on the page as if in stanzas.

It strikes me as terribly sad that some of the most beautiful writing done by Canadians is largely unknown because it happens to be tucked away in scripts that go unread. So, Amis's snide wager is, likely, a good one, but that's a reflection on us and our reading habits. It has nothing to do with any deficiency in the literary abilities of our playwrights.

Don's script is as yet unpublished and unperformed. It can *only* be treated as a piece of writing. But it is a piece of writing whose "integrity" is momentary. I am one of the few who will read this draft, and I'm reading it because I was asked for my opinion. When the play is produced, the cast, the director, and Don himself will suggest or make changes to the script. So, my comments here are a commentary on a cloud. *The Woodcutter* will become fully itself only *after* production and publication.

Still, here are my impressions. The play begins . . .

> *Dusk. A small opening in the woods with conifers — pine, spruce, fir, larch — thick all around and above it. Brief snatches of sky through branches. On the ground, brown evergreen needles, sticks, small rocks, forest debris. The end of a grey day late in October. Crows cawing, sounding both angry and annoying.*
>
>   *We hear Ted before he enters.*

> *(Off)* Are ya there yet?
> *Are ya there yet?*
> Could be just goin' round in circles anyway,
> ya stupid shit!
> Ya stupid *circlin' shit!*

Two things are given to us at once: the woods and a voice that speaks with a Canadian accent. My first thought, on reading the beginning, was of the Brothers Grimm rendered by an eastern Canadian. To be specific, I thought of Rumpelstiltskin. It's in the way Ted, the only character in this monologue, is described (short, thin, wiry, bantam . . . not a dwarf per se, but along the lines), and in the violent comedy of his entrance. He is lost in the forest, he stumbles, he swears at sticks and at the ground. In the first quarter of the play, it's possible to laugh at Ted in a way that, by the second half, becomes unthinkable. At the beginning of the play, his anger and frustration don't yet have a context, so it's possible to find Ted amusing.

Storytelling, the providing of "context," is partly (at times, *entirely*) what the play is about. Ted is fascinated by the parents of Hansel and Gretel. He recounts some of the variations he's heard, variations in which the stepmother dies and the father is left to live happily ever after with his kids. He identifies with Hansel and Gretel's father, a woodcutter who can't feed his children. He also speculates, in his way, about the inexorable endings of stories: the end will come, the end must come, but first comes the wolf, or the witch, or the terrifying things that live in the forest. Terror and desolation are the fate of those trapped in tales. And, to some extent, Ted is trapped in the worst of "tales":

257

the one about the poor having the same chances as the wealthy, the one about honest labour leading to social progress and happiness. In the world in which he finds himself, Ted can no longer believe in happy endings. The pain he has lived through and can't escape is the pain he fears his children will live through.

In a curious aside, Ted mentions the rabbits that "Tubby Thompson," a childhood enemy, had when they were kids:

> Tubby Thompson with those pens a his out the back; cute, ya think. But when they had babies, ya can't go near'm, 'cause the does'd panic sometimes, kill the litter. *Eat them even*. Strange. Animals, I mean, at times. No better'n people.

And that's it. A first hint about the connection between animals and humans: quick mention of the way a doe will eat her young to protect them from humans. With this soft knell, the relentless end of the story approaches. We are put *in loco parvuli*, in the place of the child, listening to what is, finally, an unnerving story of anger and murder. Ted, we discover at the very end of the play, has slaughtered his children to protect them from the monsters in the world, to keep them from feeling the pain he feels all the time. He has fled into the forest to await his fate.

As with all the work that fascinates me, *The Woodcutter* isn't reducible to one message or idea. It's "about" storytelling, sure, in its way, but it is also political. It's at least as political as *Muriella Pent*, but in a very different key. It focuses on the lot of the underclass. Ted is the product of group homes and welfare. He can't keep a job. He is dissociative, never really experiencing specific emotion but rather a haze of emotional pain. (His first moment of "being there" comes with the birth of his son.) His growing concern for his children begins with wanting a better life for them. His deepest despair, and his episode of unforgivable violence, comes the moment he is no longer able to imagine a better life for himself or for his children or for anyone.

Maybe the most fascinating aspect of *The Woodcutter*, for me, is its language. And that aspect of the play was made more fascinating still when I spoke to Don about it. Here's another moment from the monologue:

> Her mother, she's somethin' else, that damn thing. The mouth on her. And a real hard lookin' ticket, too. Face like a . . .
> Well, scare ya, she would.

The moustache on her!
Used ta call her *Geraldo.*

This is amusing, and it uses the word "ticket" in a way I've never heard, though "hard lookin' ticket" makes perfect — and rather beautiful — sense. But the rhythm here is almost ineluctable. It pulls you along. It's entirely *eastern* Canadian. And, while reading the play, I imagined the play could *only* be performed with the accent in which it was written.

Perhaps because I'm someone interested in "the Canadian," in things that are purely or inevitably "Canadian," it struck me that Don's language is as specific to our country as any I've ever read. While reading the play, I almost felt like I was from New Brunswick myself. But when I spoke to Don about the play's language, I was surprised at how *little* the accent mattered to him.

First of all, for Don, the play is written in a voice and accent that is *not* specific to any one place in eastern Canada. It's written in an accent and rhythm that he hears when he hears eastern voices, but it's somewhat exaggerated or particular. It's the playful "eastern" accent he and Ken Garnhum — a playwright from P.E.I. — use when they're fooling around and talking about "home." It isn't, in his terms, "real," in part because he hasn't lived in Shediac for decades and the

Shediac of his upbringing no longer exists. So, the language he hears when he writes is "impossible."[47]

Second, when his work is done by actors who are *not* from the east, it's far from certain they will manage to recreate the accent Don has in mind. When doing his plays, the actors so often produce strange, unlocatable accents that Don would rather they didn't try to reproduce the one he hears. Besides, there's nothing so annoying as an actor doing accents poorly. As far as Don is concerned, better it be done in any accent that doesn't sound false. And monologue being the most artificial of theatrical creations, it's best you have few distractions — like strange accents — to deal with.

Third, Don, as an easterner, is acutely aware that

---

47   Most writers are "infantile" in this way, I think. We hear (and usually write) versions of the language we grew up with. Writers who attempt to imitate more recent language, by throwing in current expressions or slang, can come off as forced or ungenuine. But there are, of course, exceptions — I'm thinking in particular of William Gaddis's great *A Frolic of His Own* — and, in any case, the relationship of writer to current language is subtle. There is a lovely interview with Chester Himes, in *The Paris Review*, I think, in which Himes talks about the language he used in the Harlem novels (*For Love of Imabelle, Cotton Comes to Harlem*, etc.). He expresses his bemusement at being congratulated for his fidelity to the language people actually speak in Harlem. But the Harlem novels were written in France. At the time, Himes had no connection to Harlem. He invented the language used by his characters, but his inventions were so popular even people in Harlem took them for examples of actual Harlem-speak and began to use some of his expressions. The writer's private or *inner* versions of a language do catch something and reflect it back, and readers are influenced by that reflection, positively or negatively. In that sense, language is an endless game of tennis. Which is why I hate the thought that Don Hannah's "impossible" language is not faithfully rendered.

central Canadians don't give a rat's ass about eastern Canadian culture. The more specific to the Maritimes a play is, the less chance it has of being produced in Toronto. And there are too few theatres in New Brunswick, say, for him to make a living. (It's hard enough making a living as a playwright in Toronto.) So, though the accent he hears is a kind of distillation of eastern voices, though the way he writes is *essentially* Canadian, he'd just as soon his plays were performed in whatever accent suits the cast and company.

To me, all of this is sad. Leaving aside the question of eastern Canada's cultural *non*-presence in other parts of the country, there is still the matter of theatre as the place where language, *our* language and *our* accents, should have uncontested precedence.[48] So, I find it unsettling that, for practical reasons, we will rarely, if ever, hear the plays of Don Hannah, one of our best playwrights, in the accent in which they were written.

---

48   I'm one of the many who believes that Shakespeare, or Edward Bond, for that matter, should be done in *our* accents when he's done here, not in the wandering "English" accents you sometimes hear even at Stratford — or especially at Stratford — where they should know better. This is, of course, a classic contradiction — one of the many this book perpetrates. I mean, if the integrity of the language the playwright chose is, to some extent, sacred, why should we not pay the same respect to Shakespeare as we should to Don Hannah? Why should we not do Shakespeare in his accents? The answer, sufficient for me though it may not be for you, is that we are not very good at English accents. The false note that comes through when Canadian actors imitate the RSC is grating. In betraying ourselves, we can't help but betray the play. But even if all our actors

Water

It is my fifty-third birthday (it is, at this moment, 3:15 p.m. on January 15, 2010), and I am thinking about 1976, the year I resolved to be a writer. I wonder if it was a good year for me or a bad one. Hard to say, from here.

What have I accomplished since 1976? In literary terms: four books of fiction (*Despair, Childhood, Ingrid and the Wolf, Asylum*), a play (*Lambton Kent*), a handful of libretti (*Orpheus and Eurydice, Aeneas and Dido, Waterland, Wilderness, Mnemosyne*), countless book reviews and radio scripts.

Is there anything I would save of what I have written? Yes, maybe, but I don't know what.

What kind of writer have I become? Clever, with too many ideas at times, lazy, far short of my own ideals, my literary language still unmastered.

What can I hope for?

Now, there's a question that troubles me. I've been

---

were expert at reproducing English accents, we would, in creating a space where proper "English" is spoken, create a theatre that is closer to a museum than to a place for a living art form. The vitality of the theatre is what's at issue, I think. By performing plays in our own accents, we are being more faithful to the living element in *King Lear* or *Saved*. In the same way, when the Scots did Tremblay's *Les Belles Soeurs* as *The Guid Sisters*, they were being truer to Michel Tremblay's play (as it applies to Scotland) than if they had done it in the original French. There's no reason, of course, why we shouldn't have English companies doing Shakespeare or Bond on our stages. Exchange *and* naturalization are moments in the same aesthetic mechanism.

writing — steadily, constantly — since I was nineteen. I have refused to allow myself to consider that there was anything else for me to do in this life. Back then, success meant writing; failure, not writing. But halfway or more along this road, I've begun to wonder if I was made for any of this: writing, writers, the literary life. So, what more can I hope for from the writing life? More of the same . . . done slightly better, maybe, if I persist. But persist for what reason?[49]

Have I become a pessimist, then? Am I one of those bitter old scribblers who can't stand young writers and loathes my peers?

No. Surprisingly not. Or not yet. The twenty-four years during which I've taught myself, well or poorly, to be a writer have not dampened my love for writing itself. I can, when I read a poem by Don McKay

---

49 I don't often love Susan Sontag's work, but I was moved when, after an interviewer said "I don't know how people live without writing" (a sentiment many writers express), she retorted that one can easily live without writing, that there are other arts, other ways of being in the world, and that it's fatuous to raise writing to such a level. In the last few years, I've been trying seriously to imagine my life without writing. And I can just about do it, too. I can imagine myself getting up without the itch to scribble. I can imagine myself spending a day staring at trees or listening to music. (This is more difficult because, in the end, writing is my way of communicating my enthusiasms. So, hearing music I love — whether it's Howlin' Wolf or Schönberg — naturally sends me to a writing desk.) I can even imagine myself happy with painting or music making. The thing that defeats me is reading. I can't imagine myself without books, without reading. And as, to me, reading is writing's mirror image, this represents a boundary. In the end, I am wired for reading, and, so, I am wired for writing.

or a novel by Edward St Aubyn, still feel the thrill of words properly organized on a page. And that feeling, that *thrill*, wards off pessimism. Nor is it primarily new work that moves me. In recent years, I've been inspired by Lydia Davis's translation of *The Way by Swann's*, Edith Grossman's translation of *Don Quixote*, the Pevear-Volokhonsky *War and Peace*, the poems of Tomas Tranströmer, Zbigniew Herbert, and Margaret Avison. A host of voices and sensibilities that have taken their place in my imagination.

I began this memoir with a few words about Atwood's "This Is a Photograph of Me." There is a dark aspect to the poem. I mean: what to make of someone insisting that he or she is *present*, if only the observer will look closely enough at the surface of the water where he or she has drowned? As I suggested at the beginning of this piece, there are a number of ways to interpret the poem, most of them a little bleak, I guess.

But Atwood's final insistence on *being* (on the need to say, "I am here, if you look") allows for a certain light. It's possible, for instance, to think of the water in the poem as words, to think of the lake as literature. In and amongst all literary creation, a writer can get lost or drown, but his or her voice can be heard, still living, if one listens, if one will read.

In coming to Toronto, I wanted to add my voice

to the voices of those who were writing the terrain, my country, into existence. And, on this my fifty-third birthday, twenty-four years after coming to Toronto, I've done that, whatever my disappointments or disillusion or fears for the decline of literary culture.

So, am I a pessimist? Yes, by nature.

An optimist? Yes, also by nature.

Drowned but still living is exactly how I feel.

ABOUT THE AUTHOR

ANDRÉ ALEXIS was born in Trinidad and grew up in Canada. His debut novel, *Childhood*, was a finalist for the Scotiabank Giller Prize and the Rogers Writers' Trust Fiction Prize, and won the Amazon.ca/*Books in Canada* First Novel Award and the Trillium Book Award. He is also the author of several acclaimed works of fiction, including the short story collection *Despair and Other Stories of Ottawa* and *Asylum*. He lives in Toronto.